CW01472196

LAST RIGHTS

James Green

Published by Accent Press Ltd 2018
Octavo House
West Bute Street
Cardiff
CF10 5LJ

www.accentpress.co.uk

Copyright © James Green 2018

The right of James Green to be identified as the author of
this work has been asserted by the author in accordance with
the Copyright, Designs and Patents Act 1988.

The story contained within this book is a work of fiction.
Names and characters are the product of the author's
imagination and any resemblance to actual persons, living or
dead, is entirely coincidental.

All rights reserved. No part of this book may be reproduced,
stored in a retrieval system, or transmitted in any form or by
any means, electronic, electrostatic, magnetic tape,
mechanical, photocopying, recording or otherwise, without
the written permission of Accent Press Ltd.

ISBN 9781909624580
eISBN 9781786153593

For Pat, my wife
without whom Jimmy would not have found a voice.

Chapter One

Professor McBride was expecting her visitor and didn't look up from the papers on her desk when he knocked.

'Come in.'

Jimmy Costello came in.

Middle-aged, with short, grizzled hair, he had a crumpled look despite the obvious quality of his clothes. The Professor turned a page and carried on reading. Jimmy waited. She was his boss, the woman who told him what to do, when to do it, and who he should do it to. So he waited and looked at her working.

Always the same, never any change. The same tight, curly hair, the same dark skirt, the same crisp white blouse. No. He was wrong. She *had* changed. Her left sleeve was empty and pinned up. Having your left arm shot off, that had to be classed as a change...

Yes, he admitted to himself, losing your arm was a change. But that wasn't what he'd meant. Apart from the arm, she was the same now as when he'd first known her, neat as a nun straight from the laundry. White shirt, black skirt and a brain like a bacon slicer.

The Professor turned another page so Jimmy looked out of the window. He liked the view from this top-floor office. On a clear day you could see the hills of Frascati, and today wasn't only clear but filled with morning sunlight. One day he'd keep the promise he'd made to himself when he'd first looked out of the window. He'd go to Frascati for lunch and drink their local white wine. Mind you, he'd been promising himself that for over two years, ever since he settled in

Rome, but somehow he'd never got round to it. You put things off, that was the trouble, one way and another you just put things off. Still, one day he'd catch a local bus and go and sit in the shade and drink the fresh white wine and...

He checked his watch. Time was passing.

'I'm supposed to catch a plane in a couple of hours and you know what it's like trying to get to Ciampino in a hurry. The traffic's murder. It's probably too late already.'

She looked up, waited a moment, then closed the file and gave him a wintry smile.

'No, that's changed.'

Jimmy felt a small twinge of nerves. Her smiling at him wasn't good. She'd never been one of life's great smilers.

'What do you mean, changed?'

'I don't want you to go to Brussels.'

'Good. Flying low-cost out of Ciampino wasn't exactly my idea of fun.' He tried to sound pleased.

She gave him the smile again and Jimmy felt another twinge.

'I'm sending you somewhere else. Something's come up.'

'Things do, don't they?'

Professor McBride looked at him in that way she had, tolerant disapproval.

'Brussels will have to get along without you.'

'If you say so. But you realise that without me being there, you might be risking the end of the European Union as we know it. Still, you can't have everything, can you?'

The smile went.

'Spare me your humour, Mr. Costello, and try to remember that I do not arrange these trips for your entertainment.'

Jimmy shrugged. He was used to her manner now, just like he was used to working for someone whose day job was being a college professor but who sidelined as some sort of fixer for the Catholic Church. She was the one who got handed the dustpan and brush when the carpet needing lifting so something nasty could be swept quietly out of sight, and Jimmy was the one she used to make sure the right things went under the right carpets.

It wasn't an everyday line of work, but then Jimmy didn't have everyday credentials. A working life spent as a CID sergeant in London had given him the right kind of background, although he'd never been sure whether being a bent copper with a track record for inflicting violence had helped or hindered his selection. He hoped what had really clinched it for him was his skill as a detective, but he still wasn't sure. On the jobs he'd done for Professor McBride so far he'd needed both his detecting skills and his familiarity with violence, so maybe it didn't matter. In fact it was all a bit academic, like her. Jimmy smiled to himself at his private joke.

The Professor had gone to considerable trouble to recruit James Cornelius Costello. She had arranged for him to come to Rome thinking he was going to train for the priesthood. It hadn't been hard for her because he had indeed wanted to become a priest, and had submitted an application through the usual channels in the UK. He'd wanted to do something for his wife, even though she was dead. As a widower he wasn't debarred, and becoming a priest seemed to offer the best way to make some sort of amends. Some sort of contrition. It wasn't, of course. He was and would remain what he had made himself. There was never any easy shortcut to redemption.

He'd come to Rome, to Duns College, full of hope and good intentions, but had been used by Professor McBride to get what she wanted. Of course that meant Jimmy hadn't got what he wanted, to be a priest. But there you are, he thought, in this life not many people get what they want.

Despite the way he'd been recruited, he'd done a good

3

job for her, but he'd left loose ends: dangerous loose ends, the fatal sort. To be fair, she'd helped him with all that. Found him what should have been a safe place so he could have another go at thinking about the priesthood. It hadn't been her fault it blew up, it hadn't really been anybody's fault. It just blew up. And after two goes at thinking about the priesthood he knew it would never be for him, so he'd accepted the offer she'd made to go and work for her and, insofar as he could be, he was grateful. He gave her his loyalty because she'd pretty much given him back his life. In her tangled way she had provided him with some sort of purpose, some reason to go on.

'If I'm not going to Brussels I hope it's a good substitute. Brussels sounded like it might have been worth a visit.'

'Vancouver.'

'Is that a good substitute?'

'It's Vancouver.'

'If you say so.'

Professor McBride took an envelope out of the file she had been reading and pushed it across the table to him.

'Your contact details.'

Jimmy picked up the envelope but didn't open it.

'And what do I do when I get to Vancouver?'

'You will be told.'

'Why don't you tell me?'

'Because you wouldn't believe me. You never do.'

'No, that's true.'

'But that doesn't matter because you never do what I tell you anyway.'

'Also true.'

'And be careful. I don't want a repeat of Paris. No dead police.'

'No, I don't want that either.'

'And no entanglements, not of any sort, sexual or otherwise. Remember what happened in Santander.'

Jimmy showed his surprise. 'I didn't think you knew about that.'

'Of course I knew. Where were you when it happened, by the way?'

'At Mass. It was Sunday. Who told you about her and me?'

'No one told me. A young policewoman shot in bed while naked and asleep. That sort of thing gets noticed and put in reports. It didn't need much detective work to see that you were the real target. I wouldn't have mentioned it except whatever was going on between you and her mustn't happen again.'

'It's not likely to. I still don't know why it happened there. I can't understand what she saw in me. I was old enough to be her…'

But the words petered out as the memories returned. Suarez was there again, beautiful and in control; she was looking at him across the table where they'd gone for dinner. She'd seen something in him, something he didn't understand but which had made her love him. He didn't know then what it was and he still didn't know. The next morning she was dead and now he would never know.

Professor McBride was fully aware that what she'd said would cause him pain, that was why she'd said it,. It was necessary. She waited and let him think about it. And, while she waited, she thought about it herself. An older man, not at all conventionally attractive: what *had* the young woman seen in him? But she didn't really need to ask herself because she already knew the answer. Under that exterior there was something that would be attractive to a certain type of woman, a compassionate woman, if that woman could get close. And the inspector in Santander had obviously got close, very close. Unfortunately it had killed her...

Well, it was all finished and done now. But she wanted to

make her point absolutely clear. There was to be no trouble this time.

'And I don't want to have to send any more false Vatican diplomatic passports to keep you out of jail.'

Jimmy came back to the present and nodded; she was right. What could he say?

'Look. Are you sure I'm good for this any more? Maybe I'm past it. Look at the unholy cock-up I made of the last job. I made mistakes, bad mistakes. People got hurt. Killed.'

He had a point and he could tell she'd thought about it.

'Yes, you made mistakes, and people, as you say, got killed.'

'And Copenhagen wasn't much better.'

'I disagree. One way or another Copenhagen had to happen, it was all part of the unfinished business left over from Rome. At some point it needed finishing.'

'And Lübeck?'

She shrugged her one good shoulder.

'They as good as killed themselves. Call it suicide if you like. And as for Bronski, no one could possibly lay that at your door.'

'That's true.'

'But Santander was indeed a mistake.' Jimmy looked down at his hands; she could see she'd done enough, he understood. 'See that you learn from it and don't get involved with anybody. Just get the information you need and get the job done.'

'Why not get someone fresh? Someone younger. Someone fit.'

'Physical fitness is of small consequence. It's not your body that interests me.' Thank God for that, he thought. 'All that concerns me is that you are still capable of being the detective you were. Paris was, as you say, an unholy mess, but Santander, leaving to one side the unfortunate Inspector Suarez, was a different story. You did well in Santander.'

'Maybe so, but my point is, can I still do it? There must be other detectives, good ones, who don't get people killed.'

'There are. But apart from your ability as a detective you have one indispensable asset that makes me choose to persevere with you.'

'My chirpy North London charm?'

'Your silence.'

Jimmy knew what she meant. God knew he had his faults, plenty of them, but he didn't have a slack mouth. What God also knew, however, was the real reason he could be trusted to remain silent about his work was because he didn't have a friend in the world and didn't want to make any. That was why she could rely on his silence. Not because he had any great gift for discretion but because, apart from her, he was utterly alone in the world now. No ties and no loyalties.

He slipped the envelope into the pocket of his jacket.

'When do I go?'

'You're on your way. You were packed and ready to go to Brussels, now you're packed and ready to go to Vancouver. Your ticket is waiting at the airport, at the check-in.'

Now it was Jimmy's turn to smile. Rome to Vancouver, thank God it wouldn't be budget.

'Fiumicino?'

'Ciampino.'

'Oh, no, why? Nothing goes from there direct to Canada, does it?'

'You go to London Luton and from there to Heathrow. From Heathrow you're on an Air Canada flight with a connection at Chicago. I managed to get a special price doing it that way.'

'Hell's teeth, do you realise what that journey will be like? I'll have to get a train from Luton and then get across London to Paddington for the Heathrow Express. I'll be dead before I make the boarding gate.'

'Well, it's too late to change now. I've booked your tickets.'

'Look, rather than do it that way I'll pay the difference for a direct flight.'

'And claim it on expenses when you get back? I don't think so.' Before he could get his protest out she carried on, 'You only have yourself to blame, your last claim came as a severe shock to our accounts department. I had to do a lot of hard-talking to get it passed. It's your own fault if I'm having to economise this time. Your plane leaves in two hours so you'd better get a move on. I've seen to it that someone is waiting downstairs to give you a lift. As you say, the traffic to Ciampino is always a nuisance if you're in a hurry.'

'A nuisance? You'd put it as strongly as that?'

'And you'll have to get a move on, your Air Canada flight leaves at ten p.m.'

'Anything else?'

'Just use your initiative and do the job.' Jimmy turned to go. 'And take care. I've invested too much time and effort in you to have to go looking for a replacement.'

'I'm fond of you as well, Professor.'

She didn't respond and Jimmy left the office.

Professor McBride looked at the door for a moment. Yes, she could see what might have attracted young Inspector Suarez. Underneath, and well hidden, was the terrible loneliness of a badly damaged man who would never make excuses for himself, never ask for help and never give up. She turned and looked out of the window at the distant blue hills, then picked up the phone on her desk. She would make a call. Whatever he might say about himself, she didn't want to lose Mr Costello. He was too valuable an asset, and he would be very difficult indeed to replace.

Chapter Two

Jimmy was in a foul mood as the plane descended into Chicago. The journey from Rome and through London to Heathrow hadn't been as bad as he'd expected. It had been worse. First off, it was Professor Scolari who was waiting at the reception desk where Jimmy had left his holdall. Scolari didn't like him and, to be fair, he had good reason.

'Professor McBride asked me to give you a lift.'

Jimmy tried to smile and sound grateful.

'Thanks, the traffic will be hell as usual, but if we're going to get to Ciampino in time for the flight we should...'

But Scolari had other plans. Unlike Jimmy his smile cost him no effort, but it wasn't a nice sort of smile.

'I will drop you at the nearest Metro, Mr Costello. Numidio Quadrato. I'm afraid I do not have time to act as an airport taxi.'

And that's how it had begun. The bastard knew the Metro line from Numidio Quadrato didn't get him anywhere near Ciampino. That was bad enough, but at Anagnina, the last stop on that line, he'd made the mistake of getting on the airport shuttle because it was there and about to leave. What he should have done was look round for a taxi. The shuttle stop-started through the suburbs and then hiccupped along with all the other traffic on the congested main highway for what seemed hours.

Finally he'd got to the airport and after running to the check-in desks he'd made it time. But it had been a damn close thing and that, together with Scolari's departing words outside the Metro station - '*So* glad to have been of help, Mr

Costello' - had set his nerves on edge for the rest of the journey.

Needless to say, when he arrived at Luton station from the airport there were delays and when he got on a train it was overcrowded, dirty and slow. By the time he arrived at Heathrow the place seemed to him to be a barely functioning shambles, and although the processing onto his flight had been routine and unexceptional the flight itself was over two hours late.

Once on the Air Canada plane he'd settled down. His seat was in the middle of the wide-bodied monster and he was hemmed in. All he could do was to sit and brood, so he brooded. His wasn't the sort of mind you could shift into neutral and park, so it niggled at him, building up grievances against Professor McBride, in particular the 'special price' deal that had prevented him from upgrading.

There was a wait of just under two hours for his transfer when he arrived at Chicago's O'Hare, more than long enough to get a proper meal but, even though he felt hungry, he decided against it. He knew your body went all over the place when you spent too long in the air and moved across too many time zones and he had developed his own idea of how to deal with it. Eat as little as you could on the flight, then get stuck in to whatever was the appropriate meal on arrival and carry on from there. The way he looked at it, giving your stomach breakfast when it was expecting dinner or vice-versa would be the quickest way of getting your body in line with the local routine. But he had never tested it out on a really long journey.

Instead of eating he spent the time browsing the bookstores for something to occupy his mind during the next leg of the journey. He chose a book pretty much at random, *Night Runners of Bengal*, by somebody he had never heard of called John Masters. He chose it because he liked the title and didn't much care if it was travel or fiction. He also chose it because it was, by comparison to many of the other door-stop paperbacks, slim and would slip into his jacket pocket. He also bought a copy of the *New Yorker*. Then he found himself a seat where he had a good view of a departure board, started to skim through his magazine and waited. He felt better by the time he boarded and it helped his mood considerably when he was able to get an aisle seat.

Jimmy enjoyed the book. It was easy to read, well-written and interesting, set in the Raj at the time of the Indian Mutiny. He also found two good articles in the *New Yorker*, so when the plane banked to make its final descent and he got a glimpse of the sky over Vancouver he felt reasonably cheerful. The morning looked clear and sunny and Vancouver would be a new experience, one he hoped he might have time to enjoy. He didn't know much about Canada but what little he knew was encouraging.

The plane touched down and taxied to its allotted place. Once the seatbelt lights went out the rush to get hand luggage began. Jimmy didn't normally join in this scramble, there was never any point in hurrying unless you had to. But as he was in an aisle seat he had to make way for those on the inside, he got up and, when he could, pulled his holdall from the locker and then stood and waited. *Why the rush?* thought Jimmy. Getting off the plane quickly only gave them more time to stand waiting to get their hold luggage back. When he travelled his needs never ran to more than one holdall small enough to count as hand luggage. Bernie had always been the one who made sure he looked presentable, and now she was dead he didn't much care how he looked.

The plane doors opened and the exodus began.

He felt distinctly better as he entered the Arrivals area. He had expected the usual anonymous, functional processing area, a place for discharging the stream of life that was nothing more than self-loading baggage. But this was different. It was, as far as could be achieved in an international airport, almost welcoming. It was smaller than Jimmy had expected and was dominated by a huge, elaborate totem pole. Jimmy had never seen anything like it, and he was pleased and impressed.

After taking in the totem pole he looked around to see if he was being met. He wasn't. He moved to a quiet spot, put his hand into his jacket pocket, and pulled out the envelope McBride had given him. He looked at it for a second then tore it open. Inside was a sheet of paper with a name, an address and a phone number. The name was Sister Lucy Gray SSZ. What the hell did SSZ stand for?

He looked at his watch then remembered he hadn't adjusted it. He looked around and saw from an arrivals board that the local time was just before eight in the morning. He changed his watch and pulled out his mobile. He looked at the phone number on the paper then dialled. It kept on ringing until a recording of a woman's voice cut in and asked him to leave a message. He rang off.

What now? Was it urgent, this job? McBride had pulled him off the Brussels thing at the very last moment and sent him here double quick. The way she'd done things it seemed urgent, so why no reception at this end, just a name, an address and a number that wasn't answering? McBride must have told this Sister Gray he was on his way and yet there was no-one at the airport or at the phone number. His mood soured again. It had all the hallmarks of a screw-up. But at least it wasn't his screw-up. He put away the envelope and the phone. He would go into town, get a room, have a shower, take a short rest and then try to rejoin the human race. Until he'd spoken to this Gray woman or to someone else who knew what was going on he wouldn't know anything about anything. He dismissed immediately the idea of contacting Professor McBride.

He looked around and saw a sign for taxis and headed for

it. When he got to the taxi-rank and was about to get into the taxi he realised he didn't know where he wanted to go. A hotel, obviously, but whereabouts and what sort? If he was going to have to spend time in this city he wanted to be comfortable and at a good address.

The driver was waiting patiently for a destination.

'I'm on holiday. I want a good hotel, somewhere with views and in a part of town where I can see the sights, one where I can make myself at home, spread out, not be cramped in just one room. Know anywhere like that?'

The driver turned and gave him a big smile. She seemed a friendly sort.

'Sure, you want the Rosedale on Robson.'

'If you say so.'

'I say so.'

'OK, the Whatsit on Wherever.'

The driver turned around and the taxi pulled away into the airport traffic and the morning sunshine.

Chapter Three

Jimmy hadn't slept on the plane, hadn't even managed to doze, so now his eyelids felt heavy and whatever sort of landscape he was travelling through failed to register. After a while he caught himself napping, pulled himself up in the seat and looked out of the window. The taxi was among city traffic and there were skyscrapers on either side of wide, busy roads. It was all pretty much what he'd expected, but it was only with an effort he didn't doze off again as the cab made its way through the canyon-like streets. Eventually the driver turned a corner on which stood yet another skyscraper and then pulled into a small square, drove round it, stopped and turned to Jimmy.

'Here we are, mister.'

Jimmy realised that this skyscraper was his Whatsit on Wherever. He hauled himself and his holdall out of the taxi, paid, adding a generous tip, then went into reception. Did they have a suite available?

The young woman gave him a big smile. She too seemed a friendly sort of girl.

'All our accommodation is in suites, sir, the Rosedale on Robson is an all-suite hotel.'

'Fine. Can I have one with a nice view?'

'Sure. Do you have any more luggage?'

'No, just this.'

His lack of luggage didn't seem to bother her and the check-in routine continued. When it was over Jimmy thanked her, refused help with his holdall and took his plastic pass-key. As he was about to leave, the smiling girl asked him if he wanted anything special sent up to his room? Jimmy paused; there was something about the way she'd said 'special'. Was she offering to have a prostitute sent up? It didn't look like that kind of place but how could you tell? Vancouver wasn't London or Rome. Maybe it was different over here.

'Like what?'

'You're English, sometimes our English guests like to have a toaster in their room and a teapot, you know, for breakfast.'

That got a smile out of him.

'Thanks, no toaster. I'll take a teapot though. I'll sort myself out about anything else.'

'You'll find everything you need in your suite and there's a store just round the corner, they'll have milk and everything else you might want.'

'I've just got in from Rome via Heathrow and O'Hare and currently I'm one of the walking dead. I really don't fancy shopping, even just round the corner. Could someone get me some instant coffee, milk and sugar, and tea bags if they have them? Any sort will do.'

That got an even bigger smile out of her, which wasn't what he'd expected. He'd expected a Roman response, something sub-zero which, whatever words were actually used, would mean 'do your own bloody shopping'.

'Sure, I can arrange that. I'll have everything sent up.'

He was right, it was different over here. He'd never been in a hotel where they took this much trouble - but then again, his had been a sheltered life, especially where decent-class hotels were concerned. He'd arrested people in a few, but not stayed in many.

'Thanks. I appreciate it.'

'Skimmed, semi-skimmed or full-cream?'

For a second Jimmy thought she was sending him up. Then he realised she was really trying to help.

'Full-cream.'

And he headed off for the elevator while the girl on reception picked up a phone.

Check-in had dispelled any lingering grouchiness and he went up to his suite feeling better, but still dead tired. His suite had a good-sized living room with a small kitchen area to one side, a bathroom and one bedroom. He unpacked and then took a shower. While he was drying himself someone knocked at the door. He wrapped the towel around him and went. A young man was holding a carrier bag. He held it out to Jimmy.

'The things you asked for, sir.'

Jimmy took the bag.

'Can you put it on the bill?'

'I'm afraid not, sir.'

'OK, come in.'

The young man came in and Jimmy went to his jacket which was hanging on the back of a chair. He took out his wallet.

'How much?'

'Six dollars eighty-three cents.'

Jimmy counted out seven and held them out.

'Keep the change.'

The young man looked at the money. Jimmy grinned and took out another five dollars.

'That OK? I'm not used to Canadian money yet.'

The young man returned the grin.

'That's fine, sir.' He took the money and pocketed it. 'In fact I'd say it's generous. Thank you.'

So, friendly but not dopes. Jimmy began to feel he might like Canadians if they were all like the ones he'd met so far. He finished drying himself, emptied the things out of the carrier bag and put them away. Then he went to the bedroom and sat on the bed and phoned reception for an alarm call in two hours. Two minutes later he was in bed and asleep.

He didn't know how long the phone had been ringing when it finally penetrated his consciousness. He leaned over and picked it up.

'Thanks.'

He got up, went into the bathroom and splashed cold water on his face, then came back into the bedroom. When he was dressed he went into the living room and stood at the window. His suite was sixteen storeys up and below him Vancouver was busy going about its business. He felt better, cheerful even. The taxi driver had been dead right, the Rosedale on Robson was just what he wanted and, after the journey he'd had, what he'd needed. From what he'd managed to take in of the ground floor it seemed a classy sort of place and, from what he could see down below, it looked to be in a good location. Beyond the other skyscrapers which surrounded the hotel he could see distant mountains and blue sea.

He suddenly felt grateful to the elusive Sister Lucy Gray. Not meeting him and not answering his phone call meant he had time to look around and explore. But first it was time to get himself localised, and right now he wanted to see whether his plan would work. In Vancouver it was lunchtime so his first meal here would be lunch, and the way he looked at it, his body clock would get a good kicking from his stomach if it tried any kind of grouch about what sort of meal he ate. Sort out your stomach, get it used to local-time meals straight away, and your body clock could go and whistle Dixie. Anyway, that was his plan. And he was hungry. He had eaten nothing except a few biscuits and a sandwich since leaving Rome, which meant his insides felt like one large aching void crying out to be filled.

He left the suite and headed down to the ground floor. The hotel restaurant there didn't do anything to dent the good impression the place had made on him. The food was good, the service excellent, and the staff, again, were friendly. They made you think they actually cared about whether you enjoyed your meal. Was it good employee training or were all Canadians like that, he wondered. Jimmy decided it had to be training: a country of friendly people didn't exist. How would it survive?

After his meal he went to the bar just to sit. He was tired again, he needed a couple more hours in bed to keep him going, but he wanted to think about the job before he went back to his suite. That devious sod McBride was up to something. He was sure of that because she was always up to something. If she wouldn't tell him anything at all about why he was here then it was certainly because she wanted him in Vancouver without knowing anything about the 'why'. So, if he knew nothing about the 'why', what did he know? She'd made him drop Brussels at the very last moment and rush over to Vancouver by some stupid, roundabout route. Whatever that had been about, it wasn't primarily about any 'special price' to keep the accountants happy. And why, when he got here, make him sit on his hands because his only contact couldn't be contacted? He tried to think why she would want it that way, but his tiredness kept blocking his focus on the problem. No, he was still too whacked. If his brain wouldn't work, it wouldn't, so he left the bar and made his way to his room. Five minutes after he arrived at his suite he was back in bed and once more fast asleep.

Chapter Four

There was a ringing somewhere. It woke him, he reached out for the noise and his hand found the phone. A strange voice spoke to him. It was an effort, but he managed a reply.

'What alarm call?'

Jimmy didn't know where he was or what this woman on the phone was talking about. He barely knew who he was.

'The one you ordered yesterday evening.'

Jimmy didn't remember doing anything yesterday evening but he didn't like to call her a liar.

He put the phone down and lay back. Suddenly he remembered where he was and he forced his eyes open. It was eight o'clock, time to get up and get some breakfast. If he let himself go to sleep again he knew he'd sleep until lunchtime or beyond. He struggled out of bed and headed for the bathroom. The shower helped. It only got him halfway but that was enough. He knew how to handle things now. This was something he'd done more times than he cared to remember. You'd had a long day and a harder night, surveillance maybe or a nasty collar in the small hours. You finally got to bed, knackered, and as soon as your head touched the pillow the alarm woke you and you had to begin again. By the time you left the house you had to be up for it, fit and alert on the inside even if you looked like shit on the outside. Detective sergeants couldn't afford to go on duty while they were still half submerged. Senior officers were mostly unforgiving bastards, but young inspectors were the worst because they were the ones chasing promotion and allocating blame was one of the things they did best, however many mistakes they made themselves. Tiredness or a hangover from the night before didn't count. If you went on duty you had to be ready for whatever turned up. And that was how he wanted it now, especially as he still didn't know what was waiting for him.

He dried himself, put on a bathrobe, and went to the kitchen area and made himself a cup of tea. He would drink his tea and get his mind into gear then he would go for a short walk before getting some breakfast downstairs. He looked across at the window. The sun was shining. It looked like it might be another nice morning.

When he left the hotel he found he didn't really need to be wearing his jacket. There had been rain, you could tell from the pavements and from the hanging droplets glittering like diamonds where the sun hit them, but it had stopped some time in the night and the sky was clear blue. It was autumn but to Jimmy it felt like the beginning of a fine English summer day. He set off in no particular direction. Already the place was busy, people and traffic all on their way somewhere, shops doing morning trade and food outlets serving coffee to people on the way to work. It was a big city but somehow the place still managed to have some sort of charm. He couldn't say what it was exactly but it was the same feeling he'd got when he had passed through Paris a couple of times, a sort of comfortable easiness among all the bustle. Maybe it would be a good substitute for Brussels after all. He decided he could like Vancouver if it gave him a half a chance.

After his walk, back in the hotel eating his breakfast, he turned his mind to yesterday's journey. McBride wanted him tired and harassed by the time he took off at Heathrow and she wanted him angry about her 'special price'. That had given him something to think about, something to occupy his mind during the long flight. She wanted him in a bad mood when he arrived so he wouldn't try too hard to make contact - if no-one's answering the bloody phone then sod them. Find a good hotel, Mr Costello, settle in and take your time. And she'd got exactly what she wanted, but why did she want it that way? Then his mobile rang. He took it out.

'Hello.'

'Who is that, please?' It was a woman's voice.

'It's the one answering the phone. Who are you?'

There was a pause. Jimmy was about to end the call when the voice came back.

'You aren't by any chance Mr Costello?'

Now it was Jimmy's turn to pause.

'Who's asking?'

'Sister Lucy Gray. I got a missed call message and didn't recognise the number. I thought I'd check. I was told a Mr Costello, James Costello, would be getting in touch. Are you Mr Costello?'

'Who told you to expect him?'

Another pause.

'I understand your caution if you are Mr Costello, but I can give you no further information until you confirm who you are.'

Suddenly Jimmy was tired of pissing about being careful. This was his contact, she was the only one who could tell him what the hell he was doing here.

'Sure, I'm Costello. I phoned you from the airport as soon as I arrived. I had the crazy notion I was coming here because something was urgent.'

'I'm sorry you didn't get me. I didn't know when to expect you or I would have come out to meet you, although even if I had known, well, it was one of those days. I had an early meeting and then I had to go to the…'

'Thanks, the story of your life will be fine some other time. Just at the moment I've flown six thousand miles and have no idea why.'

'I see. I thought you would have been told.'

21

'No, I haven't been told.'

Another pause. It was still early but already it was a big day for pauses.

'We should meet.'

'Yes, Sister, we should. Where and when?'

'Where are you now?'

'The Robson on, no, it's the Rosedale on Robson.'

'I know it. Could we meet in your suite? I think I would like our talk to be in private, somewhere where I'm not known and no one will see us together.'

'Should I wear false whiskers and dark glasses? Will we need a password?'

'Yes, I can see how it must seem a little excessive, but I will explain everything when I get there.'

'And when will that be?'

'How would Wednesday of next week be? I could make it at eleven.' Jimmy nearly laughed out loud. 'Otherwise I'll have to go into the following week, I'm afraid.'

This time Jimmy did laugh, but it was a laugh of anger, not because anything was funny.

'Yeah, next Wednesday at eleven will be fine.'

'Oh good, I'm so glad. I'm afraid my diary is very full just at the moment.'

'When you get to Rome you can give me a call and I'll tell you how to get to my apartment.'

And he rang off.

His anger passed as soon as he put the phone away. It was really only staged anger, enough to make it sound real in his voice. Actually he was rather pleased with it. He had never been able to act, to tell a really convincing lie, but he'd worked at it and now he felt he had a workmanlike grip on bending the truth backwards if he had to. He took a sip of his coffee. It was still warm enough to drink. He waited. Either she would ring back or she wouldn't. If she didn't ring straight back she wouldn't ring at all. If that happened he would take a couple of days to see the sights then head back to Rome.

He waited for fifteen minutes. Nobody rang so he left the restaurant and went out of the hotel to have another look around.

Chapter Five

By eleven thirty Jimmy was sitting outside a bar drinking a beer. The bar was by the harbour and overlooked the bay, a wide expanse of blue which ended in distant hills. At the foot of the hills was some sort of dark line. Jimmy had never seen anything like it and thought it magnificent. He chose the bar simply so he could sit outside looking at it.

A waiter passed his table.

'What are those big hills over there?'

The waiter stopped and looked.

'Vancouver Island.'

'And that dark line.'

'What line?'

'That dark line at the bottom where they come down to the sea.'

The waiter laughed.

'That line is Nanaimo.'

'What's that, some sort of Indian thing?'

'No, sir, Nanaimo is a city.'

'A city?'

'That's right. Not Vancouver but still a city, skyscrapers and all.'

Jimmy looked again at the 'big hills' across the bay.

'Thanks.'

The waiter moved on. Mountains, and they must be bloody massive if the buildings at the bottom looked no more than a line against them. This country was big in a way he'd never seen big before. He forgot his beer for a moment and just sat looking.

The bar was part of a waterfront which bustled with visitors and locals. Across the road at the harbour, people were pottering about on some of the boats, doing whatever people who owned boats did to them. On the decks of a couple of the bigger ones, the motor yachts, people were sitting at tables on the deck. It looked a lazy life and an expensive one. Vancouver obviously wasn't short of a bob or two.

Jimmy went back to his beer, another thing that had impressed him. It was a good pint, almost a London pint. Finding real beer, beer like you could get in England, had been a nice surprise and finding that it tasted almost as good as a London pint had been an even bigger surprise. Vancouver hadn't disappointed him so far. He couldn't fault what he'd seen and the day had kept warm and sunny. He was enjoying himself. He decided that after he'd finished his pint he would go and look for somewhere to get lunch. They would do fish round here and he liked fish. Then his phone rang. He took it out. He didn't recognise the number. It was a woman but not the woman from the morning.

'Mr Costello?'

'Who wants to know?'

When the voice spoke again he recognised the heavy Irish accent.

'God, Jimmy, you don't change do you? You're still about as polite as a dog that's had its dinner stolen.'

'Philomena!'

'How did you guess? What gave me away? Not my bit of a brogue surely?'

'God, Philomena. Where did you spring from?'

'Oh, I'm not in Canada. I'm still in Paddington, at Barts.'

'Then what…'

'Never mind any "then what". What have you been up to?'

'Up to?'

25

'Why did you upset Sr Lucy? God man, she has enough on her plate without you coming the hard case on her.'

'You know her?'

'We've met.'

Jimmy suddenly understood the mysterious SSZ after Sr Gray's name: Sisters of Saint Zita. She was from the same order as Philomena.

'Look, I got a big hurry up call from…' he didn't want to use Professor McBride's name, not even with Philomena. 'From someone and got rushed out here at very short notice. I assumed it was important and urgent, but your mate Lucy was out when I got here and then phones and offers me a slot in her diary in the middle of next week.'

'So you came the heavy. Jimmy, have you not changed at all? After your little bit of trouble here I thought you turned over a new leaf. As I remember it you went of to Rome to train as a priest. What happened to that?'

'It's a long story. I'll write a book about it one day and send you a signed copy.'

'Don't bother, the scrapes you got us through here in Paddington was story enough for me. I like it how it is now, nice and quiet.'

'Barts going well?'

'Never mind Barts. I went to a lot of trouble to find you and now that you're where I want you to be, get on and help Lucy. Never mind any more acting the clown and showing everyone what a tough guy you are.'

It wasn't a request, it was an order.

How come he finished up being bossed about by women? But she was right, he really had been a tough guy once. There had been a time in his life when he'd not have thought twice about putting someone in hospital if it was needed. So how come he rolled over like a pet poodle for Philomena and McBride? Not that the reason mattered. He did, and that was that.

'OK, what should I do?'

'Ring her now and set up a meeting.'

'OK.'

'And apologise. She's got enough on without…'

'Me acting the clown. I know, you already told me. Do I get told what this is about?'

'Did no one tell you?'

'No, no one told me.'

Another pause got added to the day's tally.

'In that case I'll leave it to Sister Lucy.' The voice at the other end became concerned. 'And take care, Jimmy.'

'I always do.' But there was something about the way she'd spoken. 'Is there something wrong, something I should know?'

'No. I'm not sure. Nothing I can tell you now over the phone. Where are you staying?'

'A place called the Rosedale on Robson.'

'I'll think about it and maybe drop you a line.' Her voice cheered up. 'Now, remember what I said, be careful, we nearly lost you here. We don't want to be losing you somewhere else.'

'We all go sometime, Sister.'

The voice went back to businesslike.

'We do, but your time isn't just yet, so get on with it and give Sister Lucy all the help she needs. Goodbye, Jimmy, and God bless.'

She rang off and Jimmy felt strangely sad as he put the phone away. He hadn't given any thought to Philomena and Barts for a long time but hearing her voice, suddenly like that, brought it all back and he realised he missed her. She was about the only person in the world he might describe as a friend. Then he knew why he had to do whatever she told him. She loved him and he loved her. You get to feel like that about a person sometimes, especially of you've saved her life and she's saved yours.

He finished what was left in his glass and reluctantly took out his mobile. Sr Gray apologised, Jimmy apologised. Sr Gray said she understood the trouble he had gone to. Jimmy said that was OK, it wasn't so much trouble. Sr Gray said she would like to meet. Jimmy said, great, but Sr Gray said she really was busy and it couldn't be before Monday morning, would around eleven be alright?

That was three days away but Jimmy tried to sound like that was fine, so he said that would be fine. Sr Gray apologised again. Jimmy said think nothing of it, he'd take in the sights. Sr Gray said it was a lovely city, she hoped he'd enjoy it. Jimmy said he hoped so too. Sr Gray began to apologise again so Jimmy said, goodbye, see you on Monday, and finished the call.

Three fucking days to sit on his arse. But then he remembered Philomena's words, so he let it go. He looked out across the harbour. Maybe Vancouver was a city worth three days, a city worth getting to know. What he'd seen already he liked. Anyway, he'd give it a good shot. After all, what else was there?

Chapter Six

Sr Lucy Gray was sitting with Jimmy in his suite. She seemed nervous.

'I'm afraid we got off to a bad start.'

Jimmy shrugged. 'It happens sometimes. Let's both forget it. Do you want a drink, tea or coffee?'

Sr Gray looked at him.

'Have you any Scotch?'

That took Jimmy by surprise. It was eleven o'clock in the morning and she didn't look like someone who hit the bottle early.

'No, sorry.'

She thought about it.

'I saw a store next to the hotel when I arrived. Why don't I get us a bottle and we can have a drink while we talk.'

Jimmy didn't know what to say. She was pretty much what he expected from a nun except she wasn't that old, late thirties or early forties. She was smartly dressed in an office kind of style, neat hair, no make-up. The only thing that gave her away was a neat little silver cross pinned on the lapel of her jacket. A Catholic might have spotted it for what it was, but to everyone else she was just another businesswoman. Jimmy was waiting for her and when she had arrived in the lobby she'd seemed reserved and a little tentative, almost shy. Yet now here she was suggesting that they should split a bottle of whisky together. It didn't add up. Or maybe things *were* different in Canada. But if they were that different, Jimmy wasn't about to adapt.

'I'll stick to coffee.'

'Oh.'

Then Jimmy remembered his orders from Philomena. He was here to help, not pass any judgement. He made the effort.

'But listen, you go ahead if you want to.'

'Really?'

'Sure.'

She got up.

'I'll be right back.'

She picked up her handbag, gave him a weak smile, and left.

Jimmy was a man who had always liked to be in control. All through his police career in London he had made sure he was in control, if not of events, then of himself. But that Jimmy, what they would now call the control freak Jimmy, had been blown away by his wife's death from cancer. All the crooked money he had made had been for Bernadette, her first and then their two children. But the children had left home as soon as they had grown up. Only after Bernie's death did it become clear to him that he had driven them away, not only from himself but from their mother too. But Bernie had stayed, only she and God knew why. Love, duty, habit? Then, suddenly and out of nowhere, she had cancer, then she was dead, and he was alone. He'd left London and the money had lain there, looked after by a sharp but frightened investment banker for whom Jimmy had once done a 'favour'.

Jimmy was rich. But the money felt like his own cancer, sitting somewhere growing quietly, making him richer, eating away at any sense of self-worth he tried to find. *Try to be the good-guy, go on, try to be someone Bernie could have been proud of. Just try. You made me and you know how you made me, and I'm still here and still growing. Remember? I'm what you wanted, what you worked for. Now I'm rewarding you for all your crookedness and violence.*

These days he tried to forget the man he'd been, put it away from him. He tried to be a clever and thorough plodder doing as he was told. He let Professor McBride do the deep thinking. She saw the whole picture. He was just a foot soldier. The last time he'd tried to play the Big Brain and work things out for himself had been in Paris when McBride was out of commission. And what had happened? He'd made the most God-almighty fuck-up and killed an innocent man in cold blood, a copper at that. No, no more in-control Jimmy. Now all he wanted was to be told what to do, where to do it, and who he should do it to. Somebody else could take the credit or the blame. If there was any money, somebody else could have it.

Now here he was in a hotel suite in Vancouver trying to help a nun who'd slipped out at eleven in the morning because she needed a bottle of Scotch. McBride had told him to come, so he'd come. Philomena had told him to help, to make no trouble, so he was trying to help and making no trouble. And Sr Gray was out buying booze. What next, wait until she was smashed and pour her into a taxi? He felt totally out of his depth. He'd travelled thousands of miles to help her and she, out of pure habit, had told him to hang about for a week until she could fit him in, so he'd popped his cork and told her to get stuffed. Then Philomena, out of the blue and all the way from London, had smacked his wrist and told him to be a good boy. And he was trying. But now it looked as if he might be dealing with a raging dipsomaniac who considered the day wasted if she wasn't immersed in the sauce by lunchtime.

An awful thought struck him. Was she the problem he'd been sent to deal with? No, it couldn't be that. He'd do as he was told, but no one in their right mind would send him to the other side of the world to play nursemaid to a dipso.

He felt trapped. Any minute the doorbell would ring and she would be back. He couldn't have felt more alarmed if an assassin was coming. He could deal with a killer, he'd done it before. But a drink-crazed nun? He thought of phoning McBride. But what could she do? Anyway, she probably knew that the nun was an alcoholic and guessed he wouldn't have come if she'd told him and she was probably right.

But then he thought of Philomena, and calmed down a bit. Philomena wouldn't have sent him to fix an alcoholic friend. She'd have got proper professional help. He calmed down and felt better. If Philomena wanted him there it was because it was something he could deal with, something that needed the Jimmy she knew from London, the Jimmy people tried to kill but ended up getting killed themselves. The old Jimmy, the tough-guy. But if she knew anything and was willing to tell him then she would have told him yesterday and she didn't.

Here he was, six thousand-odd miles from home, in a hotel in a strange city with a woman he was supposed to help. He didn't know why she needed his help, all he knew was that she was out buying Scotch at eleven in the morning. So he waited. What else was there to do?

Chapter Seven

After a while there was a gentle knock. She was back. Jimmy opened the door and she came in, walked to the table and put a brown paper bag on it. While she took off her jacket and hung it over the back of a chair Jimmy went and got her a glass. He put on it the table beside the paper bag then sat down. She took a half-size bottle of Scotch out of the bag, opened it, and poured a stiff measure into the glass. She looked at him.

'None for you?'

Jimmy shook his head.

She sat down, took a long drink, then pulled a face and began to cough, in between coughs gasping for breath. Jimmy looked at her as she tried to get her breath back, there were tears on her cheeks now. If you're an alcoholic, he thought, you're not very good at it.

Sr Gray held her throat for a second while her breath got back to normal.

'I think I should have put some water in it.'

Jimmy got up and held out his hand.

'Here, let me.'

She gave him the glass. He took it to the tap in the kitchen area, put in plenty of water and brought it back. She thanked him and took a cautious sip. This time it seemed to go down OK.

'Thank you, that's better.' He got the weak smile again. 'I'm not used to it.'

Jimmy's surprise showed in his voice. 'Then why did you get it?'

'I needed something to steady my nerves. I feel rather nervous and not a little stupid. I have to tell you, Mr Costello, that I was not looking forward to this meeting. In fact I was… am, a little afraid.'

'What of?'

'Well, you partly.'

'Me? You don't know me.'

'Yes, but I know something about you.'

'From Philomena?'

'Yes.'

'I see. What did she tell you?'

'That you saved her life and solved two murders. That you killed a gangster, one who was trying to kill you and her. That you were someone who understood violence and could be violent if necessary. She didn't try to make you sound like a frightening person but, well, from what she said…'

'I see.'

Sr Gray tried to rally. 'But most importantly she told me that you were an excellent detective.'

She took a sip of her drink and put the glass down on the table.

'Shall I freshen that up?'

'No, that was plenty. I told you, I only wanted to…' She looked at Jimmy's face then smiled. 'What did you think?'

'That you were a raging alcoholic who couldn't get to midday without hitting the bottle.'

She laughed.

'Oh dear, yes, I suppose it must have seemed a bit odd, coming here to your suite this morning then rushing out and buying a bottle of Scotch. I can see how you might have drawn that conclusion but I assure you it was just nerves. If I drink at all, which is not often, I drink wine, or maybe a beer to be sociable.'

Jimmy decided it was time to get down to situations. He

34

didn't want to be rude but if this thing was to get going someone had to start.

'Fine, you like wine and the occasional social beer, you're not an alcoholic, when you're nervous and a bit frightened you buy whiskey but you're not used to it, and Philomena told you a few things about me. Now do you think we could get to the part about why I'm here?'

'Yes, of course.' She made a visible effort. 'Someone has been killed. I think there's been a murder.' Getting that out seemed to help. 'In fact I know there's been a murder, no, not know in the sense that I'm certain, that I have information I could lay before the police. I have no evidence, at least nothing I can show anyone. When I say that I'm certain I mean... well, actually I don't know what I mean. Mr Costello, I need your help. Sr Philomena said you would help me.' The question was in her eyes as much as her words. 'Will you?'

Jimmy thought about it and what he thought he didn't like. Then Philomena's voice came back: 'Just get on with it.'

He tried his best to make his smile look genuine, he was better at it than he used to be, but it wasn't easy.

'Of course. It's why I'm here.'

Whether it was the words or the smile he didn't know but she seemed to relax. Maybe the Scotch had kicked in. Whatever it was, she was herself for the first time since she had arrived.

'I run an Outreach Programme and a chaplaincy. I operate from an office at St Nicodemus church. The funding comes from my order, the diocese and the government.' She paused. 'Not that any of that matters, I suppose.'

She stopped and looked at her handbag for support.

This is going to be an uphill struggle, thought Jimmy. He tried to get her back on track.

'Don't worry about how it comes out. Just talk it through,

we'll put it together in the right way later on, just talk and let yourself get where you're going. And don't worry about me, I have nothing but time.' He tried to lighten things up. He beefed up the smile into a grin and hoped it didn't look like a leer. 'I have nothing in my diary until Wednesday of next week, when I have to meet a nun,' he nodded to the bottle, 'and we still have your whiskey, so take all the time you need.'

There was nothing weak about the smile this time. She seemed to pull herself together and suddenly looked a little more confident and almost in control.

'As I told you, I run an Outreach Programme and a chaplaincy. There was a young man who came to the chaplaincy, a third-year student at the university. He was studying Art History. He wasn't a Catholic but he came anyway,' she paused, 'not that you have to be a Catholic, there's no...' Jimmy could see she was in danger of conking out again. He heaved a mental sigh.

'Go on, you're doing fine.'

'I'm not, I'm doing dreadfully. Now you can see why I was nervous, why I needed the Scotch.' She glanced at the bottle. 'Not that it seems to have done any good. I'm sitting here telling a complete stranger who I've made travel all the way from Rome that I think someone's been murdered and I'm making an awful mess of doing it. I don't know what you must think of me.'

Just as well you don't know, if it wasn't for Philomena I'd probably have thrown you out by now, was what Jimmy thought. What he said was, 'Do you want another drink?'

'God, no, if one won't help, more would probably make me worse.'

Jimmy got things going again.

'What sort of bloke was he, this student?'

'He was a happy sort and a good mixer, and he seemed well adjusted not in the least neurotic, not in any sense uncomfortable with who he was. Then he committed suicide. At least that's what the police said, suicide. But they're wrong, Mr Costello. Marvin didn't commit suicide, he wasn't the sort.'

'How can you be sure, are you an expert?'

'No.' She paused to think about it. 'Or maybe I am. I might be, if being an expert means having to be able to make judgements about the emotional and mental state of others, others who can have had stressful experiences and suffer from emotional conflicts. I have no clinical training but I have my Outreach and chaplaincy training and I have my experience. Regrettably, in my line of work I am not a complete stranger to suicide and those who exhibit suicidal tendencies. Marvin Brinkmeyer certainly wasn't suicidal.'

'Maybe something happened, ditched by a girlfriend, money problems? These things happen and young people respond in ways you and I might find hard to understand or explain.'

'Marvin didn't have a girlfriend, he wasn't in any kind of relationship - not a sexual one anyway. And he had no money problems. His parents were wealthy and as far as Marvin was concerned, generous.'

'Maybe it was drugs...'

'Mr Costello, I wouldn't have brought you all this way if I wasn't certain Marvin Brinkmeyer was murdered.'

'OK, you're convinced. Convince me.'

Chapter Eight

'Marvin Brinkmeyer didn't commit suicide because he was about to become a Catholic. He had been receiving instruction from a priest friend of mine and was due to be baptised the week after he died. He was excited and happy about it. And if that isn't enough then I can tell you that the reason he wanted to be a Catholic was because he wanted to apply for training for the priesthood. We talked about it a lot. He wanted to become a Dominican, he had actually stayed at a Dominican priory a few times. He had been told that there was a very good chance he would be accepted if he applied for training. He was a happy, well-adjusted young man who knew what he wanted to do with his life. I talked to him the day before he died and he was full of the future, he was looking forward to it. He was definitely not suicidal.'

She stopped and looked at him. Jimmy waited then realised that was it.

Jimmy turned it over in his head. A student tops himself, a nun doesn't want to accept it, so he gets dragged halfway round the world. It wasn't his idea of a sensible use of his time but he pressed on.

'Have you spoken to the police?'

'Yes.'

'And?'

'They're sticking to suicide.'

'Has anyone else questioned the suicide that you know of? The university authorities, friends?'

'No.'

'Then I don't see what I can do. I have no status of any

kind so I can't just pop up in Vancouver and start my own investigation. Why would anyone co-operate even if I did? I can't talk to the police, because you say, other than your own judgement of him and his state of mind, you have no evidence. I don't see what you think I can do.'

'I've thought of that, I discussed it with Sr Philomena. Whoever killed Marvin must be connected with the university or the chaplaincy.'

'Why?'

'Because who else is there? Marvin had his studies at the university and his social life was bound up with the chaplaincy. There was nothing else. There has to be a connection.'

'Only because you say so.'

'I knew Marvin very well, believe me, there was nothing else.'

'What about his family?'

'He never spoke of them and stayed in Vancouver during vacations.'

'You said they were wealthy.'

'Did I?'

'Yes, wealthy and generous.'

'I must have assumed that. Marvin seemed to have plenty of money. He didn't have a part-time job like some students. He dressed well, owned a car, travelled. I assumed his parents gave him an allowance, a generous one.'

'But he never spoke of them?'

'No.'

'Doesn't that seem odd to you? Wealthy parents who are generous to him yet he never mentions them and doesn't go home to visit during the vacations?'

'Yes, now you've pointed it out I suppose it is odd.'

'Maybe that was the reason. If he'd rejected his parents or they'd rejected him that might have been what it was all about.' That stopped her dead in her tracks. 'On the outside he's a normal, happy kid but inside there's something eating away at him which he's buried deep down and won't confront. One day it surfaces and, bingo, he's dead.'

'No, you're wrong.'

'Why?'

'Because he didn't own a gun. They say he shot himself but he had no gun.'

'Are guns so hard to get in Canada? And if they are, he only had to pop across to America. The way I hear it over there they give them away with breakfast cereal.'

'It wasn't a handgun, it was a shotgun. It was fired while the barrel was in his mouth and blew part of his head off.'

They both sat in silence for a second, Sr Gray unable to imagine what that must have looked like and Jimmy able to picture it all too easily. He'd seen shotgun deaths in his detective days and they were never pretty.

'Look, Sister, he puts the gun into his mouth and blows his head off. It *has* to be suicide, it can't be anything else if that's how it happened.'

'That's what the police said.'

'And they were right.'

'No, they were wrong and you're wrong. Sr Philomena believed me, why won't you?'

'Because I'm not Philomena.'

She just sat and looked at him. Inside his head the voice still said, 'Get on and give her the help she needs.'

'Why did Philomena believe you?'

'I don't know, but she did.'

Shit, thought Jimmy, there's nothing in this, just a bit of wishful thinking. It's a waste of my time. Then he suddenly changed his mind.

'OK, I agree with you. There's something to look into, there's more to this than a tragic suicide.'

The surprise showed on her face. 'What made you change your mind?'

'I haven't. I still think it's suicide but now I think it's not just suicide.'

'I'm sorry, I don't follow you.'

'Philomena didn't send me, she got someone else to send me and if I'm here it's for a reason. I'm here to look into something and it must be connected to your student's death.'

'What sort of thing?'

'I don't know.'

She looked puzzled for a second then she brightened.

'Actually I don't care, so long as you look into it and find out what really happened.'

'We still have a problem. How do I get to talk to people? Like I say, I can't just pop up and start asking questions.'

'Philomena and I worked that out, you'll be on a placement with me. You'll be training to run a lay chaplaincy and you came here to work alongside me.'

'That's no good, I wouldn't know how to do that. People would see through it in a second.'

'Why? You worked in the refuge Sr Philomena runs. That was social care.'

'I was a cleaner and handyman.'

'Not according to Sr Philomena.'

'Anyway, don't you have to be a nun or a priest to be a chaplain?'

'There are lay chaplains these days and you did go to Rome to train for the priesthood, Sr Philomena told me you did.'

'Yes, but it turned out to be a mistake.'

'But you went to Rome, you even came here from Rome. We could say that you found you didn't have a vocation for the priesthood so you decided to do Church social work and become a chaplain.'

Jimmy didn't like it but he could see it made some sort of sense. It would stand up as long as no one looked too closely, and it would put him alongside the people who knew the student, it was somewhere to start.

'OK, I'm your assistant learning the ropes. How many students come to the chaplaincy?'

'Not many, just a few.'

'A few? You run a full-time chaplaincy for just a few students?'

'No.'

'No?'

'No. It's not a student chaplaincy. Weren't you told what I do?'

'No.'

'I run an Outreach Programme and chaplaincy to the gay community, to people who are homosexual, bisexual or transsexual.'

Jimmy was too stunned to say anything or even think anything for a second. Then his brain kicked in and the penny dropped.

That was why McBride had kept him in the dark and fucked him about on the journey. She knew damn well that if he had been told he was going to work alongside a load of queers, fairies and bloody sexual perverts he would have told her where to stuff the job. She'd made sure he was drawn into the whole thing in such a way that he couldn't back out. God, she was a devious bitch.

Then he calmed down. Well, she'd got her way as usual. Here he was. The question now was, what did he do about it?

Chapter Nine

The following day they had arranged to meet at ten thirty, when Sr Gray would drive him to the chaplaincy. Jimmy was in his suite waiting and on the phone to Rome.

'If I had told you, Mr Costello, would you have gone?'

'Not bloody likely.'

'And if Sr Lucy Gray had met you at the airport and explained…'

'I would have been on the next flight home.'

Professor McBride laid on the shocked indignation with a trowel.

'Don't tell me you're homophobic, Mr Costello, that you're prejudiced against people just because their sexual orientation is different from your own?'

Jimmy took the mobile away from his ear and looked at it for a second then put it back. Somehow he could never get angry over the phone.

'Look, I don't like sexual deviants. If that makes me homophobic then, yes, I am homo-bloody-phobic. And the reason I didn't tell you how I felt about that sort of thing was because I never got the chance, did I?'

She couldn't keep the smug satisfaction out of her voice.

'Well, now you're there you must work to overcome your bigoted and un-Christian attitude. Think of it as an opportunity to grow spiritually and morally, an opportunity to mature areas of your social development which are still rooted in the Catholicism of your London-Irish childhood.'

'Leave Kilburn out of it.' McBride waited while he thought about things. 'It's important, is it?'

'Yes.'

'And it has to be me?'

'It has to be you.'

'And working with this Gray woman is the only way in?'

'You working with Sr Gray is the only way that I could see, and believe me, I looked. I guessed how you'd react and if I could have got you on the inside of this in any other way I'd have done so.'

Jimmy believed her, up to a point. She never told an outright lie, but she could and did bend the truth to get the same result.

'When did Philomena get in touch?'

'She began looking for you about three months ago immediately after she had attended a conference in Dublin, Catholic Care in the Wider Community. On that conference she shared accommodation with Sr Gray. Sr Philomena was to give a paper on her work in Paddington and Sr Gray one on her work in Vancouver. They were from the same Order and had mutual friends so sharing a room seemed the sensible thing. They obviously talked about their work and Sr Gray's problem with the young man must have come up. Sr Gray needed help and Sr Philomena thought of you and after she went back to London she began to make enquiries. I, of course, followed up on why someone was looking for you. When I found out who it was I contacted Sr Philomena. She explained and I agreed to get you to go to Vancouver and meet with Sr Gray.'

'That's a lot of effort just because an old friend of mine makes enquiries about me. There must have been something else, something to make it worth your while shoving your oar in.'

'I already knew about the young man.'

'That he'd committed suicide?'

'Yes, and that Sr Gray had been to the police claiming it was murder.'

Jimmy lined it all up and the light came on.

'It was all a bloody set-up.'

'Of course it was.'

'You wangled them both onto that thing in Dublin and saw to it that they shared a room because you guessed they'd talk about the suicide and wanted Philomena to contact me to help.'

'Good heavens no, I couldn't leave it to chance. They might have talked about anything.'

'Then how did you make sure that...' The light grew brighter and Jimmy saw it all. 'Of course, you were there, you wore your college professor's hat and made sure you got invited. You stage-managed the whole thing. It must be very bloody important if you set up a whole ruddy conference.'

'No, I merely adapted an existing one so that it would suit my purpose. I arranged to be invited to give a workshop on the Social Manipulation of Poverty by Government Agencies in the Developed World. It actually is rather a pet subject of mine. I also arranged for two places to suddenly become available and Sr Philomena and Sr Gray to be offered them. All expenses were paid and qualified relief staff supplied to cover for them so they were happy to come at short notice. I spent quite a lot of time with them both and we spoke a great deal about the tragic death of the young man and what Sr Gray might do.'

'How come you knew about the student?'

'About a month before he died he stayed for the weekend at a Dominican priory.'

'Sr Gray told me he was thinking about becoming a priest.'

'A friar, Dominicans are friars.'

'Whatever.'

'He asked one of the friars what would happen if it turned out that the Church owned stolen art treasures. He

45

said it was for a book he was thinking of writing, a crime-thriller with an art background.'

'But the friar didn't believe him.'

'He had his doubts.'

'Which he shared with someone else, and finally you were told to sort it out.'

'I was asked to look into it. Maybe there won't be anything to sort out. Who knows, perhaps he really was writing a novel.'

'What about the suicide?'

'What about it?'

'According to the Gray woman he blew his head off with a shotgun. It has to be suicide.'

'Does it?'

'For God's sake, don't go all fey on me. Did he kill himself or was he murdered?'

'Mr Costello, why do you think you're in Vancouver? If I could answer your question with any certainty I wouldn't need you there. Just get on with it, get the job done.'

'What job?'

'Find out what the student knew, if anything. See if there's any truth at all in it. If there is, try to find a way to...'

Jimmy waited but the phone remained silent.

'Tidy things up?'

'To do whatever is necessary. I can't allow important stolen art works to turn up in the possession of the Catholic Church. The media would have a field day.'

'And we wouldn't want the Church to look bad in the media, would we?'

'If there's anything to it, sort it out. If not, come back. Just get on with it.'

And the phone went dead.

'Get on with it.' Now there were two of them at it. Well at least now he had some sort of idea what it was he was supposed to be getting on with. Suicide or murder and an outside chance of stolen art, stolen serious art, the sort of art that puts the wind up people who know about art. He put away his phone and looked at his watch. Ten fifteen, time to go down and wait for the Gray woman to arrive.

Jimmy sat in the hotel's main entrance. He wasn't looking forward to the day. Going undercover among a bunch of queers wasn't his idea of…

He stopped. If he thought like that it would never work. But that was *exactly* how he thought about it, they *were* a bunch of queers. Changing the name to gay didn't change anything. They were still a…

No, this was definitely not going to work. But what alternative did he have? Come on, Jimmy, you're supposed to be the great detective, think of something.

About five minutes later Sr Gray walked in and came over to him.

'Ready?'

He got up.

'No.'

She gave him a surprised look.

'What's the problem?'

'You are.'

'Me?'

'Come on, let's go up to my suite. We need to talk and this time I'm the one who could do with a Scotch.'

He turned and headed for the lift. She followed him.

Chapter Ten

Jimmy had a whisky on the table beside him. Sr Gray was sitting looking at him, waiting.

'It's not going to work.'

'Yes it will, all you have to do...'

'I can't work with a bunch of queers.'

He could see her freeze.

'I see.'

'No, you don't see, so I'll try to tell you. You probably won't understand but I'll try anyway.'

Her words when she spoke had icicles on them.

'Thank you.'

'Don't thank me, I'm not doing it for you. I'm doing it for Philomena.'

'OK, explain to me for Sr Philomena's sake why you can't work with me and, using your own words, a *bunch of queers.*'

Jimmy ignored the tone.

'I can't because that's how I would be thinking. When I was a copper I never worked undercover so I have no training or experience and if, in my head, that's what I'm thinking, how long would the charade last? Feeling like I do is not something I can help, it's the way it is, the way I am. And even if I could pass for someone learning to work with people like that, it still wouldn't work because how I feel, how I was thinking, would get in the way of what I needed to do. My judgement wouldn't be just clouded, it would be crippled. I'd balls it up and get nowhere. I was a detective for over twenty years, I know how these things work. I'm 'not guessing about this, I know.'

He took a drink and waited.

'Is Sr Philomena a lesbian?'

Whatever he was expecting it wasn't that and he resented the question. Somehow he felt it was a personal insult.

'No, she bloody isn't.'

'And exactly how do you know she isn't? Did you ask her or did she tell you? Or did you do some detective work and find it out for yourself?'

Jimmy didn't answer. There was no answer, but he could see she was going to wait for one. She was going to sit and look at him until she got an answer of some sort out of him so he did the best he could, but he wasn't happy about it.

'It never came up.'

'I see. According to Sr Philomena you solved two murders and killed some gangsters who were trying to kill you both.'

'I only killed one, or, if you want the accurate truth of the thing, I had him killed.'

'One, then. I should imagine while all that was going on you and Sr Philomena became quite close.'

'Yes, I suppose we did.'

'But her sexuality never came up?'

'No.'

'But mine and that of the people I work with matters from day one?'

'It matters, so why not from day one?'

'Do you assume that I'm gay because I work with gay people?'

Jimmy shrugged. She was a nun, in his book nuns didn't have sexuality. They were just nuns. But he was beginning to suspect that his book might be an old one, a child's one, one that he'd been given as a boy in Kilburn but somehow kept on using all his life.

'And because of that assumption, which is based only on

your own prejudice, it's the first thing that comes up. And you haven't even met any of the people I work with, let alone killed anyone yet.'

She was different today, that much was sure. Jimmy was the one who needed the whiskey. He took another drink.

'I told you, I can't help the way I feel.'

She paused.

'Tell me, Mr Costello, did you ever arrest a paedophile?'

'Two.'

'And if they had said that they couldn't help the way they felt, would you have accepted that as a defence or a justification?'

Shit. He'd walked right into that.

'No.'

'But I'm supposed to accept it in your case?'

Put like that he could see what she meant. Suddenly she seemed to thaw.

'Look, Mr Costello, I'm quite used to people who share your opinion and often express it in stronger terms or even violence. But I thought I was getting a trained detective who could put personal considerations to one side. If you could explain why you think working alongside gay people would somehow impair your…'

'I once put a q…' he managed to catch himself, 'a homosexual in hospital. I kicked the shit out of him and nearly killed the bastard. Not long after that somebody did kill him.'

She sat silent for a second.

'I see.'

'No you don't. Denny Morris was scum, a villain who no one in the law could touch. I found he was putting kids on the street, boys of no more than eleven. When I tried to nail him I was warned off.'

'By his gang?'

'By a detective inspector speaking on behalf of a senior

officer. Denny was plugged in all the way to the top. Anyway, I found out that he was using the kids himself before he put them on the street. He was a… for God's sake, he was a fucking bastard. There's no way I can call him gay. Denny Morris wasn't gay. He was an animal. He kept it very quiet, being homosexual, but a young bloke he'd used, used and hurt and I don't mean emotionally, told me, in return for getting him off a drugs charge. But I vowed I'd get the bastard one day and, like I say, one day I did.'

'Mr Costello, paedophiles are not exclusively homosexual, and I would guess most gangsters and pimps are straight, not gay. Having a sexuality which has been traditionally condemned by society doesn't turn someone into a monster like your Denny Morris character. I'm sure you must have known some gay men and women who were not animals, not fucking bastards, who could, in a dim light, pass for normal people and who didn't produce in you the urge to put them in hospital.'

Jimmy thought back. Offhand he couldn't think of anybody he'd known well who was gay, but some of them could have been.

'When I was young it was illegal, a crime. That sort of sets your mind in a way of thinking. Back then nobody let on if they were that way inclined.'

'That's a long time ago. Things have changed, thank God.'

'Maybe so, but I haven't changed with them. I suppose it's my fault but it never came up so I never thought about it and I guess I'm still stuck where I started. I remember the first time I came across one. I was a young copper and I saw this bloke hanging round some public toilets that were on my beat. He was an older, smartly dressed sort, looked liked an accountant or something. I told him to move on. "Go on, bugger off," I said. I remember he gave me a funny sort of smile and said, "But, my dear boy, that's exactly what I'm trying to do," and went on his way. I remember thinking he seemed a harmless sort of cove. But I soon learned you can seem a harmless cove and still be a criminal.'

Jimmy took another small drink then pushed the glass away. It was all out in the open now so he didn't need it any more. It hadn't helped much and he still didn't like whiskey.

'So, where does that leave us, Mr. Costello?'

'Look, even if I could do what you suggest, it wouldn't work. I have to ask questions, to interview people. I get what I need by talking to people and getting them to talk to me. I need those people to trust me, to tell me things they might not want to talk about. Look at us two, how well did we get on?' He could see she took his point. 'OK, it wouldn't be as bad as that but it wouldn't be good enough either, not if I'm pretending to like them and work with them.'

'I see.'

'But I have a suggestion.'

'Well?'

'If I was representing the parents of the student that died, then I could ask questions, make some sort of proper investigation. People would be willing to help if I was trying to find out why he died, if I was doing it for the parents. How I might feel about anybody, well, it needn't come up. If the people who knew him liked him then we'd all be doing it for him, for his parents.'

'It's a great pity you didn't think of this straight away. If you had then there would have been no need to go through…'

'Yes there would, because I would still have had to make you understand how I think about it all. My boss is the devious one, not me. We'll need to work together on this which means we've got to trust each other. I trust you because Philomena thinks you're OK. You didn't know anything about me except what she told you and that made you reach for a bottle of whiskey. Well, whatever she told you is over, it's all true, but it's all in the past. Now I work for a college professor, I try to sort things out and she tells me which things to sort. But I thought we should get how I feel out in the open. I didn't want you to make any mistakes about the sort of person I am.'

They sat in silence for a moment, each with their own thoughts. It was Sr Gray got things going again.

'Thank you. I appreciate your honesty. So, what do we do now?'

'You do nothing unless you have contact details for the parents.'

'No, I told you, he never spoke of them. He did tell me that he came from Seattle though.'

'Fine, that gives me a place to start. You get on with your work and I'll find out how to get in touch with them. If it works out I'll let you know.' They both stood up and went to the door. 'I'll be in touch.'

Once she was gone Jimmy went across to the window and looked out. The sky was getting dark with clouds, the good weather was gone and it threatened rain. It definitely looked like rain.

Chapter Eleven

'Is that Mr Brinkmeyer?'

'Who is this?'

'My name is Costello, James Costello.'

'And what can I do for you, Mr Costello?'

'I'm trying to contact Marvin Brinkmeyer's parents. He was a student at Vancouver University.'

The other end went silent for a second.

'In connection with what?'

'It's concerning his death.'

'Where are you phoning from?'

'Vancouver, the Rosedale on Robson hotel.'

'How did you get this number?'

'It's in the book, there aren't that many Brinkmeyers in Seattle. This is only my second try.'

Another pause.

'You will have to speak to my wife. Wait please.'

Jimmy waited until a woman came on the phone.

'My husband tells me you wish to speak to us about a student's death. That you think we might be his parents.'

'Yes.'

'You're wrong. We have no son. Goodbye.'

And the phone went dead.

Jimmy held it for a moment then put it down. They were the parents alright. It wasn't just the, "We have no son," it was the way she said it, like she was spitting it into the phone. Whatever had been the cause, the family bust-up must have been pretty spectacular. But it gave him a good line of enquiry: the money. Marvin had money, enough to dress well, run a car and travel, Gray said. So, if Mummy and Daddy didn't give it to him, who did?

OK, now he had a lead to follow. But he had also lost the best way of following it. He couldn't very well represent the parents if, as far as they were concerned, they had no son, dead or alive. Representing the parents had been his best chance to get into this thing. Well, Mummy had blown that out of the water. Now what? The Gray woman would have to be told. He picked up the phone again.

'Bad news, Seattle won't play ball.' He listened. 'Because as far as they're concerned they have no son, and I doubt it's because he topped himself. I think whatever it was it happened well before that, maybe even before he came to Vancouver... No, I'm not sure, but the mother was quite clear about not having a son and that's not how mothers usually take losing one, even if the cause is suicide... No, I have nothing else to suggest.' He knew what she would say next and she did. 'No, we can't go back to that. I told you why it wouldn't work and it still won't work.'

He waited while she tried to think of something else. After a moment she came up with something. Not much, but something.

'OK, I'll try, but don't expect too much. You get as many of them as you can and when they're set up I'll talk to them. Sure, the chaplaincy's alright. I'll be interviewing them because they knew Marvin Brinkmeyer, not pretending I'm one of them. There's a big difference, believe me.'

He put the phone down. There was nothing for him to do now except wait until Gray could set up meetings with any chaplaincy users who had known Marvin and would talk to him. He looked at his watch. It was ten past twelve, not time to eat yet. He wouldn't want lunch for a while. He decided to go down to the waterfront bar where they had the good beer. He went to the window and looked out. The rain was still coming down heavily. He would need an umbrella and maybe he should buy himself a mac.

Down in reception they lent him an umbrella and told him the nearest place to buy a raincoat. It was about five minutes away. He decided he'd go and get his beer first and pick up the raincoat on the way back. The city had changed for him, it still looked good even in the rain, but the feel was different. He'd seen places before where the surface was all smiles and friendliness, but underneath, under the surface, that was a different story. Maybe Vancouver was like that. Maybe when you got to know her well enough she was just another whore, only with classier make-up.

He sat in the bar looking out over the bay. The big white ferry which ran across the bay to North Vancouver had just pulled out from the nearby terminal and was heading towards a grey curtain of heavy rain that sat under a leaden sky and had already made the distant mountains across the bay invisible. Here though, the rain was not much more than a heavy drizzle and there were still plenty of people about though now under umbrellas or in raincoats. Jimmy sat at a table outside the bar, under an awning, and watched the world go by. The beer was still good and he had nothing special he wanted to do so he let his mind drift.

If McBride knew about Marvin Brinkmeyer's suicide it meant he must have been connected to something important, important to the Catholic Church, something they wanted hushed up and sorted out. And if McBride had been called in it meant that someone high up at the Vancouver end had contacted Rome. Who? Well, certainly not some Dominican friar that Brinkmeyer dropped a casual question to about stolen art. That set his mind off in another direction. Was there any stolen art? Or was that another of McBride's little red herrings to put him where she wanted him to be?

He looked out across the bay. The ferry was almost invisible now, the heavy rain must be getting closer. He took a drink of his beer. He was getting nowhere and he would continue to get nowhere until he had something more in the way of hard information. So far all he had was Brinkmeyer's suicide, and that had to be suicide because no one lets you put a loaded shotgun in their mouth so they can blow their head off. Do they? No, they don't, it had to suicide. So why did the kid top himself?

What if Brinkmeyer was involved in something that had gone pear-shaped and didn't want to face the consequences, prison perhaps, or answer to the sort of friends who would do nasty things before they killed you in their own nasty way. That was possible, he'd known people get into situations where blowing your brains out was the best option available. So what could he have been involved in? Jimmy gazed at the rapidly disappearing ferry while he went through the usual list of things that lead to a sticky end for those who don't know how such things work. But it was all too vague: money, drugs, sex, blackmail, what? Of course it might not be anything criminal. If Brinkmeyer went to the chaplaincy it meant he was queer so he might have killed himself because he'd been thrown over by a boyfriend, despite what the Gray woman thought. Or could it be just sex, sex with a child, the kind of molestation that got you serving a long prison sentence if the other cons didn't shorten it for you. What about money? Gray said money wasn't a problem for him, that he had wealthy parents who were generous. And he remembered the mother's voice: 'We have no son'. If Marvin was getting money and plenty of it then it certainly wasn't coming from Seattle, so where was it coming from?

Jimmy decided he'd get himself another beer, he felt he deserved one. He had a question that gave him something to do. It wasn't much but it was progress. Where did Brinkmeyer's money come from? Who was being generous to him and why?

His phone rang. It was Gray.

'OK, three of them? Beginning at twelve thirty tomorrow. Listen, why don't I start with you before I see them? We haven't gone over everything you know about Brinkmeyer yet. Sure, now is fine. How do I get there? OK, I'll see you in as long as it takes to rustle up a taxi and get there.'

He put the phone away and went into the bar.

'Another beer.'

The girl behind the bar pulled another pint and put it on the bar in front of him. Jimmy paid.

'How do I get a taxi?'

The girl pulled a card out of a wad that sat in a glass by the till. It was a taxi firm's card. Jimmy took it and his beer and went to a table, inside this time. He phoned for a taxi and told them the chaplaincy address, then put the card in his pocket and took a drink. He'd do the interviews for Gray, talk to whoever she wheeled in front of him. It was nothing more than going through the motions, a few interviews which wouldn't get him anywhere, but it would make it look as if he was trying.

While waiting for the taxi to turn up he went back to thinking about Brinkmeyer and started back on his list. The money thing was OK but did it mean you should give up on everything else. Sex? If it was just sex, even queer sex, McBride wouldn't have been brought in. Unless the person Brinkmeyer was having it with was someone high enough up to do serious damage to the Church. Was that a possibility? No, that didn't work. There'd already been too many of those sort of sex scandals for one more to matter. So not sex, not consensual sex at least. What else? These days did students blow their brains out because they were likely to fail their course? Maybe they did. These days kids at college were all nutters one way or another: 'I'm going to fail my course, oh, God, I'd better end it all.' Well, it would be easy enough to check if he was failing. But if that was all it was then why McBride's interest?

He looked out of the window again, but the heavier rain had made landfall and was throwing itself against the glass, making everything blurred. The big white ferry was gone. His mind went back to the money angle. How well did the guy live, how much did he spend? Following the money was never a bad idea. He smiled to himself, maybe these chaplaincy interviews might be of some use after all. If they knew Marvin they'd be able to fill in something of his life-style, habits and how he spent his time and money.

A taxi pulled up and the horn blew. He took another big draught of his beer, left the bar and hurried through the rain into the taxi.

'They told you where you're going.'

The driver nodded and pulled away. Jimmy sat back.

The only thing he had to go on other than Brinkmeyer's death was the stolen art, if there was any art stolen. McBride used him like a bloody sniffer dog, she gave him a smell of something and then watched him go. Still, why not? Follow the money and keep an eye out for the art and leave the sex to… Shit. He'd left the hotel's umbrella in the bar. Never mind, he thought, pick it up next time I go for a pint. If it's still there that is.

Chapter Twelve

St Nicodemus church, to which Sr Gray's chaplaincy was attached, was in a part of the city where smart apartment blocks mixed with prestigious office blocks. At street level there were shops, bars and all the other places which serviced such a mix. The church itself was a modern affair, concrete and angular with coloured glass, and stood back from the road behind its own car-park which, although it was a weekday, was full. Jimmy guessed that parking in the neighbourhood was only had at a premium and the church rented out its space when it didn't need it for Mass-goers on Sundays.

The taxi pulled into the car park and drove to the church's entrance. Jimmy paid it off and looked around. By the church doors was a small sign. On it he saw *Chaplaincy Entrance* and an arrow pointing to the right. That direction took him round to a building behind the church, a much older, brick-built affair. It had that grim, Victorian ecclesiastical look and Jimmy guessed that this had once been the church and that the modern affair was its replacement. He smiled to himself as he walked past the arched windows with their dark stained glass to the corner of the building, round which would be the main doors. I may be out of date and old-fashioned about these people, but at least I'm not on my own, he thought. They keep them round the back, out of sight, and let them use the leftovers.

When he turned the corner the frontage changed dramatically. The dark wooden doors he had been expecting weren't there. They had been replaced by a first-floor frontage that was all stainless steel and smoked glass. If you didn't look up at the stone statue of some saint who gazed out into nowhere from his niche above the doorway you might have been standing at the entrance to a small but prosperous business, probably in the financial line. It was all very solid and secure but with the understated elegance that spoke of money.

Jimmy pushed at the door gently. It eased silently open so he went in.

Once inside he stopped. He had expected something shabby and makeshift, done on the cheap with hand-me-down furniture and fittings. A run-down church interior with cold tiled floor, peeling paint and the plaster near the floor blistering from the rising damp. God knows he'd seen enough such places in his time.

What he got was a state-of-the-art conversion which would have graced anything the City of London might have done inside some venerable, old and cherished exterior. He was looking at a severe-chic café-bar area, with a mixture of easy chairs and settees beside wooden coffee tables and upright chairs at gleaming steel tables. There were small vases on all the tables, with little bunches of flowers in them. They looked real. The lighting owed nothing to the stained glass windows which had been retained, but cleverly reduced to the function of self-lit artworks and now had a beauty and appeal which they could never have hoped to achieve in their days of out-and-out holiness. Everything was bright, clean and comfortable; an upmarket bar, a place the right sort of people could come to and relax in. The sort of place that wouldn't really welcome those from the margins of society - or the Jimmy Costellos of this world.

A young man was sitting in one of the easy chairs reading a newspaper. On the coffee table was a beer bottle, a half-full glass and a plate of sandwiches. At an upright table a middle-aged man and a young woman were talking, both with dark suit jackets over the backs of their chairs. Two coffee mugs stood among the documents that spread across the table and by each chair was the inevitable black computer bag. A pair of business lunchers. At the far end of the room was the bar. At a table near the bar there was an elderly lady talking to the man behind the bar. The lady stopped talking as the man looked at him. Jimmy crossed the room to the bar. The man gave him a big smile. Jimmy didn't return it. The man was about his own age, wore a white shirt, a dark bow tie, and was wiping a wine glass with a cloth. He looked like a normal barman. But that didn't mean anything.

'Mr Costello?' Jimmy nodded cautiously. 'Please go up. Sr Lucy is expecting you.' He pointed with the wine glass to a staircase on one side of the room. 'Her office is up those stairs. You can't miss it.'

Jimmy forced out a 'thanks' and went to the staircase. The elderly lady resumed her conversation with the barman. Nobody else took any notice of him. The staircase was satin stainless-steel again but with thick hardwood steps. As he began to climb the stairs the main door opened and three more people came in talking and laughing. Two men and a woman, all young, all wearing dark suits and looking like executives. Jimmy went on up the stairs.

It wasn't the hole-in-the-corner outfit he'd expected and if the downstairs was anything to go by, the Outreach Programme and chaplaincy were certainly funded well enough. Sr Philomena in her run-down dump in Paddington would have given her eye teeth to get a place like it.

The corridor on the first floor had a thick, neutral carpet and the glass door said *Office*. Underneath it said *Sister Gray, Administrator*. Jimmy knocked and her voice answered.

'Come in, Mr Costello.' Sr Gray was sitting at her desk, a Scandinavian-style affair with an open laptop on it. 'I presumed you would prefer to talk here rather than downstairs. We can get quite busy at lunch sometimes.' She got up and went across to two easy chairs either side of a coffee table and sat down. Jimmy joined her. 'Would you like a drink, tea, coffee?'

'No thanks.'

'Wine, beer? I can get Norman to bring up anything you'd like.'

'I've just had a beer in a bar. I'm fine.'

'Very well. What can I tell you?'

Jimmy felt unsettled by everything he'd seen. Suddenly he was the one who felt like an outsider, like he didn't belong. And how could an Outreach centre like this get busy at lunchtimes? What was this district, the bloody queer quarter? Or did they travel? Then he saw that Sr Gray was looking at him, waiting. With an effort, a big effort, he pulled himself together and began.

Chapter Thirteen

'When did you first meet Marvin?'

'About eighteen months ago. He came with another student.'

'Were they,' Jimmy searched for acceptable words, 'in a relationship?'

'No. Laura wasn't his girlfriend, just a friend from the university. He was in a relationship though. That was why he came. He wanted to end it and his partner wanted it to go on. He came to ask advice.'

'Why you? Isn't there a university chaplaincy?'

'Yes, and he used to go there, but he didn't want to discuss it with any of the university chaplains.'

'Why do you think that was?'

'I got the very clear impression that his lover was a member of staff at the university. He never actually said it was, but that was my impression. If I was right then I can see how he wouldn't want to discuss it with a university chaplain.'

'So he got a friend to bring him here to get advice about breaking off an affair?' She nodded. 'And what advice did you give him?'

'I wasn't much help. In situations like that you never can be. One wants it to end, the other doesn't. There's no easy answer.'

'Did he tell you why he wanted to end it? Was it something to do with becoming a Catholic, was that why he came to you? Had he decided he should sign up to the Church line, that being gay is wrong?'

'That is not what you call the Church line. Being gay is not wrong. The Church simply says, as with straight people, that the use of sex in any relationship should…'

'I know what the Church says and you can weasel round it all you like, you still get the same message, gay is wrong. Nobody bothers with the small print.'

Sr Gray gave up trying to explain. He wouldn't listen and he didn't care. And he was right. What mattered to him, and to her, was not a discourse on Church teaching but finding the truth about Marvin's death.

'He was thinking about becoming a Catholic and had talked to the Catholic chaplain about it quite a lot. He had no problem with being gay and he thought gay people should express their love sexually. The reason he didn't want to be in a relationship was because he felt his life was moving in a new direction. He thought he might have a vocation.'

'The priesthood?'

'It was only a possibility at that point but one to which he had given serious thought.'

'So he was going to toe the Church line?'

'Yes, Mr Costello, he was, but not the line you're thinking of. He wanted to know if he was capable of living a celibate life, whether he was strong enough to live a life without active sexual expression. If he could he would go ahead and see if he had a vocation to the priesthood. If not he would drop the whole thing.'

'About being a priest?'

'About becoming a Catholic. It was a priest or nothing for him. He wouldn't have become a Catholic knowing that he intended to continue to express any loving relationship he found himself in sexually. He felt that if he became a Catholic he would have to accept the Church's teaching. If he wasn't called to the celibate life then to live that teaching as a lay person would be a denial of who he was and who he wanted to be. He was a very honest young man and also a very well-adjusted one.'

'So what happened?'

'I told him to be as honest with his partner as he was being with himself. If the other person cared about him, loved him, he would accept what he wanted to do.'

'And did it work? Did he end it?'

'He ended it but it didn't work as I had hoped. He didn't tell me the details but it turned nasty. Scenes, threats, talk of self-harm. Frustrated lust can be an ugly thing.'

'So, if he was going on with becoming a Catholic and this priest thing, as far as you know he had decided to give up sex?'

'I assume so. That was what he told me he would do.'

'Then what we have is one angry, male ex-lover who got ditched around eighteen months ago.'

'You could put it that way.'

'Then that's the way we'll put it. Were his studies going well?'

'Oh yes, he was doing very well. He had been asked to consider staying on for a doctorate when he graduated. He was something of a star.'

'Stars fall.'

'Not this one, he was gifted and he loved his subject.'

So much for the failing student idea.

'What else can you tell me about him?'

She thought for a second.

'Not much. Since I've talked to you about him I've come to realise I didn't know him very well at all. I don't think I can actually tell you much more than I already have. When you come down to it, all I knew of him was that he seemed a happy, well-adjusted young man, a successful student and someone who had discovered the Catholic faith and thought he had a vocation to the priesthood.'

'But you talked?'

'Oh yes.'

'What about?'

'When we talked, it was usually about the Church, about becoming a Catholic. It was like I told you, he was very happy with his life and looking forward to the future.'

'I see.'

'And art.'

'Art?'

'Art was the only other thing we talked about. He liked to talk about it, especially Renaissance paintings, that was something of a speciality of his. He loved Renaissance religious art. Actually it was the one thing which I found a bit trying. I like art well enough but there is a limit to how much I want to hear about it and Marvin went well past that limit on more than one occasion. The only person who seemed as fascinated by the subject as he was a man called Somerset, Thurlow Somerset. But he was an art dealer so I suppose...'

'An art dealer?'

'Yes, a very successful one. At least I think he must have been successful. He was quite rich, perhaps even very rich.'

'How did he fit into things?'

'Thurlow? He started coming about three years ago.'

'Was he a regular at the chaplaincy, a friend of Marvin?'

'No, he wasn't a regular. He came to Vancouver twice a year for about two or three weeks and while he was here he came to the chaplaincy. I think he and Marvin just enjoyed talking about art. While he was here they saw quite a bit of each other but they never seemed to be friends, more two people who shared a passion.'

'But no sex, you think?'

Sr Gray almost sighed.

'No, Mr Costello, with gay people, as with straight, it doesn't always have to end up in bed. The passion they shared was for art, not sex, at least not with each other. Gays can have friends like other people, you know.'

'You're sure this Somerset was gay?'

'I assume so.'

'Could coming here have been a way to meet Marvin?'

'Oh no, I don't think so. No, I'm sure not. Mr Somerset came twice a year and had been here about three times before Marvin turned up.'

'Why did this Somerset come to Vancouver?'

'No idea. Business, I suppose.'

'Where did he come from?'

'New York. That was where he said his gallery was.'

'And what did he talk about when he wasn't talking art to Marvin?'

'Religion, the Catholic Church. What it was all about. Obviously we talked about the Church's teaching on sex and sexuality but he seemed interested in all aspects of the Church. He had an almost voracious appetite for knowledge, nothing about the Church was too obscure or difficult or remote. He seemed to want to know everything.'

'He wasn't a Catholic?'

'No.'

'Was he thinking of becoming a Catholic?'

'No, I never got the feeling that was what he was looking for.'

'What do you mean, looking for?'

'He seemed to be trying to find out something. It was as if he believed the Church was keeping some sort of secret, some knowledge which he wanted to share.'

A slight eagerness crept into Jimmy's question.

'A secret? Something to do with a Catholic church here in Vancouver?'

She gave a small laugh.

'No, the Church in general. There was something about the faith of Catholics he wanted to discover. It was quite disconcerting. I told him what I could, answered his questions, and he'd think about it, think about it very carefully. The next time we spoke he either wanted to look at whatever it was more deeply or he had sort of swept it aside and started looking again. But I honestly have no idea what it was in the Catholic faith he was looking for. Marvin might have understood. Maybe it was something to do with art and I missed it.'

'How come this Somerset bloke was allowed to come to a Catholic chaplaincy if he wasn't a Catholic?'

'You don't have to be a Catholic or even a Christian. Some come with their partners because the partner is a Catholic, some come because they want to feel part of a worshipping community, not shut out from the world of people of faith. Some come because they want to be accepted for who they are but not join in the more aggressive or assertive ways of doing so.'

'Sorry, can I have that in English?'

'They didn't want to use gay bars or clubs.'

'I see. So this place was a sort of acceptable low-level version?'

'No, it isn't.'

Jimmy didn't understand but he pressed on.

'Does the bishop approve of this chaplaincy?'

'Yes, without Church approval I couldn't and wouldn't be doing this work.'

'But if the people who come here are actually...'

He still had to fish for words which wouldn't offend so Sr Gray helped him out.

'In sexual relationships?'

'That's definitely against the rules for Catholics, so doesn't this chaplaincy seem to sort of approve of Catholics who break the rules?'

'I don't ask what the nature of anyone's relationship is, and people, quite sensibly, don't volunteer the information.'

Jimmy understood that alright. It sounded like it used to be in the Met: 'Don't tell me and I'll not ask, that way we all stay happy.' Only in the Met it wasn't queers, it was villains, and the relationship wasn't sex, it was money, and plenty of it. Jimmy knew, he'd made enough himself while his colleagues turned a blind eye.

'OK, we'll leave it there for the time being. Who am I seeing tomorrow?'

'There's Laura, the student who first brought Marvin. She's very keen to meet you and help. Then Peter, he's a music teacher, and Anton. He's an actor, when he's working that is. At the moment he's in telesales.'

Jimmy stood up.

'Fine. How do you want me to do it?'

'Do it?'

'The interviews.'

'How would you normally do it?'

'One at a time, in here at this desk. I'd want you present.'

'Oh, I don't think that will work.'

'Why not?'

'Peter and Anton are going to be here on their lunch breaks and they only have an hour. Including travelling. You'll have about half an hour for both, so if you talk to them one at a time I don't think you'll get very far. Laura's a student, so depending on lectures she could come earlier, I suppose, or later.'

Jimmy didn't care. They weren't going to tell him anything except background stuff. They weren't a priority. The art dealer was the one he wanted to talk to now. McBride had said it was about paintings, so an art dealer popping up couldn't just be a coincidence. That had to be where McBride wanted him to get to, and she wanted him there without anyone else getting even a whiff of stolen art. Credit where credit's due, he thought, she's a devious bitch but a damn clever one.

'OK, I'll see them all together. That art dealer, Somerset... What did you say his first name was?'

'Thurlow.'

'How would I contact him?'

'I'm afraid I've no idea except that he's from New York. Do you think he might be important?'

'No, but I like to keep track of everything. OK, I'll be back tomorrow for twelve thirty.'

She stood up and held out her hand.

'Thank you, Mr Costello. I feel so much better now someone is looking into this.'

Jimmy took her hand and tried to smile but it didn't take so he gave up. 'Pleased to be of help.'

'I'll walk down with you.'

They left the office and at once Jimmy noticed the sound of voices coming from downstairs. Once on the stairs he saw that about half the tables were occupied. There must have been about thirty people there.

Sr Gray must have noticed the surprise on his face.

'No, Mr Costello, these people aren't part of the Outreach - at least, a few of them are, but not many. It's just that this is a popular place for some of the office workers to take their lunch. It's comfortable and we do an excellent light menu.'

'Oh, I see. I thought…'

'I know what you thought, Mr Costello, but you were wrong.'

They reached the front door. 'Please understand, Mr Costello, I *do* appreciate your helping in this and, for what it's worth, I think I know what an effort you are making.'

There was nothing Jimmy could think of to say so he pulled the door open and left.

Outside he felt better. He was getting back to the world he knew, a world he could deal with. OK, he'd been wrong about the people having lunch. But he wasn't wrong about Brinkmeyer's suicide, and he wasn't wrong about Thurlow Somerset being the reason he was here. About those he was he was right, right on the button.

Chapter Fourteen

'Mr. Costello.'

The voice carried across the hotel lobby as Jimmy walked towards the lifts. Jimmy looked across to Reception. The young man behind the desk beckoned to him. He went across.

'Yeah?'

'You have a message. A Mr Brinkmeyer called and asked that you should be told that he will call again. He said you'd know what it was about.'

'Thanks. What time did he call?'

The young man checked a slip of paper.

'Two fifteen, forty-five minutes ago.'

'Did he leave a number?'

'No, but he said that if you were out when he called he would call back regularly until he got you. I guess it's important.'

'I guess it must be. Thanks.'

Jimmy went to the elevator.

So, perhaps Pa Brinkmeyer wasn't the hard nut Ma Brinkmeyer was and he cared about how and why his son died. Jimmy went up to his suite, made himself a cup of tea and sat by the phone. He hadn't been waiting many minutes when it rang. It was Brinkmeyer.

'Good afternoon, Mr Costello, thank you for taking this call. I'm sorry about what happened when you called this morning and I would like to explain, but not over the phone. Could we meet?'

'Sure, where and when?'

'Would you mind if I first ask you how you are involved with my son's death?'

'Sr Gray asked me to look into it. She doesn't think it was suicide. Do you know Sr Gray?'

'My son spoke of her, he thought highly of her and the work she did, but we never met. You say Sr Gray asked you to look into my son's death. Are you a detective?'

'No, not a policeman of any sort. I'm a friend of a friend.'

The voice took on a doubtful tone, as if Brinkmeyer was thinking the call might have been a mistake.

'I see.'

'No you don't and I can explain, but I don't want to explain over the phone either. If you want to meet we'll meet. I'll tell you why I'm involved then. If you want to, you can tell me your side of things.'

Brinkmeyer brightened.

'Thank you. Can you come to Seattle? I'm afraid it's impossible for me to come to Vancouver and I have to fly out to India the day after tomorrow.'

'How long would it take for me to get to Seattle?'

'If you fly you'll be here in less than an hour. I could meet you at the airport.'

Jimmy worked out times.

'I've got meetings tomorrow at lunchtime. I'll leave tomorrow afternoon. I don't know how often flights are. I'll have to…'

'I've checked.' There was a pause while he must have looked at something. 'There's a flight at four twenty. Could you make that?'

'Yes.'

'It gets in at five ten.'

'Fine, how will we know each other?'

'I'll have my driver waiting outside Arrivals displaying your name. He'll bring you to the car and we can talk while he drives around.'

'Fine, I'll see you tomorrow.'

There was a short pause.

'Thank you for what you're doing, Mr Costello.'

'Keep the thanks until you know what I'm doing.'

And Jimmy put the phone down.

If Pa Brinkmeyer hadn't given up on his son, and it looked like he hadn't, then that would explain where Marvin's money came from. Was that good or bad? Jimmy wasn't sure. If it was coming from his father it meant the money was straight and that closed down his most promising line of enquiry. But if Pa Brinkmeyer wanted to talk that put representing the parents, or at least the father, back into the frame. And there was still Thurlow Somerset.

OK, that was tomorrow sorted, interviews at lunchtime then a plane to Seattle in the afternoon. Now it was time to go out, have a beer or maybe two, take in some sights and look around for a place to have dinner. Somewhere down by the waterfront again. He liked the waterfront. He would go somewhere and have fish. He would find somewhere he could get something really special. It was just a feeling of course, he couldn't be sure, but he felt this town was going to be good to him if he gave it half a chance.

Chapter Fifteen

Next morning Jimmy stood drinking a cup of tea by the window of his suite looking out over Vancouver. The sun was shining again. The previous evening he'd found a restaurant on Coal Harbour Quay which was in a great location, overlooking the water. He'd eaten wild salmon that had been baked on a cedar plank. It was good, he'd thought, not great, but definitely on the good side. Tonight he would try somewhere else and have something different. Maybe he would have a look at Chinatown. He was enjoying discovering a new city, the more he found out about it the more he liked it. His mobile on the coffee table began ringing. He looked at his watch. It was eight thirty.

He went and answered the phone.

'Yes.'

'Who is speaking, please?'

'It's the man who's answering the phone. Who's that?'

'This is the Vancouver police.' The voice let it sink in, then continued. 'Would you tell me your name, sir?'

The voice was extra-polite but behind the politeness Jimmy recognised a copper who wanted to know something and knew how to get told, so he didn't try to mess about.

'Costello, James Costello. What's this about?'

'Do you know a Sr Lucy Gray?'

Jimmy put his cup down. He knew what was coming from the tone of the voice but he still went ahead and asked.

'Is she alright?'

'I'm afraid not, sir.'

'How bad is it?'

'Sr Gray is dead.'

'An accident?'

'We cannot comment on the cause of death at this time.' Jimmy didn't say anything.The voice waited then went on. 'We would like to talk to you, Mr Costello.'

'Sure. I'll get a taxi to your station. Where are you based?'

'If you don't mind, we'd like to come and talk to you. Where are you staying?'

'I'm at the Rosedale on Robson. When do you want to come?'

'We'll be with you around ten if that's OK.'

'That's fine.'

'Thank you, sir.'

And the phone went dead. Jimmy put the mobile down and went back to the window but he wasn't thinking about the view. This was turning nasty. A student blowing his head off was one thing. Nuns getting killed was something else. Was it tied in to the Brinkmeyer thing? He was fairly sure it had to be. Shit, if this was dangerous, McBride should bloody well have told him.

He made a call. It was answered as soon as it rang. Did McBride live in her office?

'The Gray woman is dead. She died some time last night.'

'How do you know?'

There was no surprise or even concern in McBride's voice.

'I've just had the police on. Did you know something like this might happen?'

'No.'

'Did you think it might?'

'No.'

Jimmy persisted, you had to nail her down tight to get anywhere.

'Did you have any idea at all that there could be violence?'

'No, none at all. It appears I have underestimated the situation. How are your enquiries going?'

If Gray's death had had any effect on her she was doing a first-class job of hiding it.

'I'm not sure. I've turned up an art dealer from New York who knew the suicide. Is the art dealer where you wanted me to get?'

'Yes.'

'And you couldn't just tell me?'

'You needed a reason for being there and asking questions and you had to be convincing. If you arrived and started asking questions about the art dealer you would have got nowhere, believe me. This way, my way, you've been asked by a friend in London to help out with a student's death which may or may not have been suicide. Sr Philomena will back up that story and so will Sr Gray,' she paused, 'at least she would have if she hadn't…'

There was a pause so Jimmy finished the sentence for her.

'Died.'

'Mr. Costello, I regret the death of Sr Gray, it is most unfortunate. But I don't want the art side of this to get into anyone's hands, not anyone at all beyond those who are already involved. It could be most damaging.'

'And how many are there, already involved?'

'That we know of, I count four so far, don't you? Sr Gray, Sr Philomena, the art dealer and you.'

'And you, which makes five, and whoever got you involved, six, and whoever told them, seven, and…'

'Mr. Costello, no good purpose will be served by your being facetious. What else have you done?'

'I've arranged to fly down to Seattle this afternoon to meet the dead kid's dad and I was supposed to meet some people who knew Marvin at lunchtime today although I doubt they can tell me much that will be of use.'

'See them anyway if you can. Even if they have no worthwhile information it will help your cover story. Well, it seems you have got to where I wanted you to be. From now on it's up to you.'

'What about the Gray woman?'

'What about her?'

'I'll tell you what about her. The police are coming here to interview me this morning about her sudden death. If it turns out she's been murdered you can forget the whole thing. I'm on the first plane back to Rome. Two people involved in this have already died, I don't want to be next.'

'There will be no next. Brinkmeyer committed suicide and we don't know yet how or why Sr Gray died. Whatever happened to Sr Gray I doubt anything will happen to you.'

'Oh you doubt that, do you? Look, I was the one who got a knife stuck in him in Santander where there was going to be no violence. I'm not taking any chances of a repeat.'

'Sr Gray's death is regrettable and was quite unforeseen, but she had served her purpose as far as our involvement is concerned so it need have no further bearing on the matter. See the young man's friends, meet with Mr Brinkmeyer, then there's one more thing I need you to do in Vancouver. When you've done that I want you to go to New York and see the art dealer and get the job finished.'

'You're a cold bitch, you know that?'

'Vulgar abuse will help neither of us, Mr Costello. The job needs doing and, as always, you've made an excellent start. Just keep on and get it done.'

There it was again – get it done. Suddenly Jimmy was tired of being pushed.

'And if I don't?'

'Then I may have to make a call to someone and inform them that unfortunately I am no longer able to guarantee your continued discretion. I'm sure you understand.'

There hadn't even been a pause for thought, she had the answer right to hand. She'd obviously given it some thought.

Jimmy didn't say anything straight away. Would she really do it? If she did he was a dead man. Would she hand him over to the Israelis? She didn't kill people and, if you put aside her methods, he'd always looked on her as being on the side of the angels. But he couldn't put aside her methods because he was one of them, and people did get killed even if she didn't do the killing.

'You really mean that? You'd give me to the Israelis?'

'Why say it unless I meant it?'

Jimmy had known since the Copenhagen business that she could get him by the balls any time she wanted. It was only now he understood how strong her grip could be when she did. He gave up. It was a doubt against a certainty, he might get hurt if he stayed, but he'd be dead if he left and went back to Rome.

He'd stay, but he'd be very careful and take no chances.

'OK, I'll see what I can do but I'm not sticking my neck out. What is it you want me to do here before I hop off to New York?'

'Make an appointment to see a Mr Felton Crosby, he works for the Vancouver Diocese. Wait one moment and I can give you his number.' Jimmy waited until she came back on and gave him a number. 'I will speak to him so he will be expecting you. He will tell you how this all started.'

'And will that be everything?'

'No, not everything. If I had everything I wouldn't have needed to send you, would I? But once you have spoken to Mr Crosby you will know as much as I do. After that I expect you to find out if the paintings really are stolen masterpieces as Brinkmeyer said. If they are, I need to know how the Church got involved and how the matter can be satisfactorily resolved.'

'And the Gray woman?'

'Leave it to the police. It's none of our business.' Jimmy didn't say anything. 'I mean it, Mr Costello, don't get side-tracked. Remember what I said to you before you left Rome, stick only to the job in hand.'

Jimmy put the phone down and waited for a while. It didn't ring. He took a drink of his tea. It was cold so he took it to the sink and poured it away. Then he phoned reception.

'I'm flying to Seattle this afternoon at around four, for a meeting. I'll want to come back this evening. Could you find out if there's a flight I could get?'

'Certainly, sir.'

'Fine. I'll get some breakfast and then pick up what you've got.'

He thought about the call from the police. They must have got his number through Gray's mobile. All they would want to do was check him out. He wouldn't have anything to worry about from that quarter. He was a friend of a friend doing a favour. It would be the truth, it just wouldn't be the whole truth.

He went down and had breakfast, then went to reception.

'There's an Air Canada direct flight at seven thirty-five or a Northwest flight at eight fifteen. After that…'

'That's OK. One of those will do fine. Thanks.'

Jimmy went back up to his suite. In less than an hour the police would be knocking on his door. He knew what he would tell them but he still had a lot of thinking to do. If the Gray woman's death turned out to be murder then whoever did it was involved with Brinkmeyer and the stolen art. The art was what it was all about and it was serious enough for Marvin to kill himself and maybe for Sr Gray to get murdered, if she was murdered. But if he wanted information quickly about how Gray died the only people who could tell him were the police. He needed to think of some way of interviewing them while they were busy interviewing him. And he had to believe in what he was doing, if he tried to put on an act then… well. Like McBride had said often enough, they both knew what sort of actor he was. So Jimmy went to the window and started thinking.

Chapter Sixteen

'Can we go over it again, Mr Costello? You have a friend in London, Sr Philomena McCarthy, who contacted you and asked you, as a favour, to come to Vancouver and look into the death of a student, Marvin Brinkmeyer?'

'No, let's get it right. I obviously haven't made myself sufficiently clear. Sr Philomena was at a conference in Dublin with Sr Lucy Gray. Sr Gray told Philomena about the suicide of someone she knew, Marvin Brinkmeyer. Sr Gray was worried and felt that the death was suspicious, that it had been pigeonholed as suicide too quickly by the police and that their conclusions might have been wrong. Philomena wanted to help so she said she'd try to find me. As it happened I now live in Rome and I know Professor McBride of the Collegio Principe in Rome, I do jobs for her occasionally. She was giving a paper to the conference. The three talked. Sr Philomena asked Professor McBride to ask me if I would come across to Vancouver and see what I could do. She asked, so I came.'

Jimmy had guessed it was going to be hard to sell them the story and he'd been right.

There were two of them, one about forty and a young one of about late twenties. The older one was Detective Inspector Brownlow and the younger one had been introduced as Detective Constable Liu. Liu didn't look Oriental, Jimmy thought, but the fact that he'd sat there and hadn't said a word since they'd come into the suite gave him an air of inscrutability, or maybe he was just imagining it. Either way it was the older one who was doing all the talking.

'That's quite a set of coincidences, Mr Costello, the three of them being on the same conference.'

'Not really. They all work in the same field and the Catholic world isn't so very big when it comes to academic conferences. Philomena and Sr Gray were members of the same Order. It would only seem a bit far-fetched to someone who didn't know the Catholic Church from the inside. Are you Catholic, by the way?' The policeman ignored the question and waited, obviously unconvinced. 'If you have any doubts about it then check it out. Get in touch with Sr Philomena in London and with Professor McBride in Rome and ask them. Check out the Dublin conference with the organisers and see if all three were there.' Jimmy thanked God that while McBride might be devious she was also thorough. The story did indeed sound goofy, but the details would stand up to any sort of check, and that was what mattered. 'I really am trying to help, Inspector. I don't like my story any more than you do, but unfortunately it's the truth, the only story I've got, so I guess I'm stuck with it.'

And Jimmy sat back.

The inspector glanced at Liu, who said nothing and went on being inscrutable. The inspector got going again.

'What exactly do you do for this Professor McBride?'

'I do odd bits of research for her. Nothing very academic, background stuff on people and places mostly. Routine plodding, times, dates, the sort policemen are used to and supposed to be good at.'

'Private detective work?'

'No, mostly from archives. Could this bloke have been in this place at this time?'

'Sounds like private detective work.'

'Yes, except that the bloke could be somebody like Henry Teonge, the place might be Aleppo, the date 1675. That was one I did for her about three months ago. She didn't think the travel arrangements of the time allowed what he'd written in his diary to work, that he'd maybe fiddled his dates a bit.'

Jimmy knew the question about his relationship with McBride would get asked so he was ready. He added thanks to Wikipedia alongside those to McBride.

'I see.'

Inscrutable suddenly came to life.

'We will do as you say, Mr Costello. We will check what you've told us and check thoroughly.'

The older detective nodded. 'Yes, we'll check.'

And Inscrutable went back into neutral.

Jimmy felt a little uncomfortable. He was fairly sure he could deal with the older one but this young bloke might take a bit of handling. Always beware of quiet coppers. If they're not talking they're thinking and you do well to ask yourself what is it they're thinking about?

The older man resumed with, 'How did you come to know this Sr Philomena?'

'I was on a placement?'

'What sort of placement?'

'I was thinking of becoming a priest, it was a pastoral work sort of placement. As you can see it didn't work out. I went to Rome for training but gave it up after a year. I liked Rome though and stayed on. That's how I came to know Professor McBride. '

'And why exactly did your friend Sr Philomena think you could turn up anything by looking into the death of Marvin Brinkmeyer? Have you any experience of police work?'

'For thirty years I was a copper in the Met in London. For most of them I was in CID and made it as far as detective sergeant. I took early retirement, stress, you know, it gets to you. But to help a friend of a friend, well you know how those things are. You feel obliged, and I've always wanted to see Canada. It wasn't that I thought I could do anything about the suicide, more an excuse to come over here and take a holiday. I've already discovered your waterfront down by the ferry terminal. There's a bar there that does a pint that would do credit to London. And last night I went to a restaurant on the Coal Harbour Quay where -'

But the older policeman didn't want any more from Jimmy's travel brochure.

'What did Sr Gray tell you about Brinkmeyer's death?'

'That he was a happy, well-adjusted young man who was about to become a Catholic and wanted to be a priest. He was looking forward to the future and was not in the least suicidal.'

'And what did you think?'

'That it was wishful thinking on her part. She liked him so she couldn't accept the idea of him putting a shotgun in his mouth and blowing his head off. The police must have come to the same conclusion when she went and told them what she thought.'

'And did you tell her what you thought?'

'Yes. I didn't use the words wishful thinking but I made it clear that I thought it had to be suicide.'

'And?'

'She asked me to talk to a few people who knew him. I'm supposed to be meeting three of them today at lunchtime, twelve thirty. I doubt it will get me anywhere. I have to say though, as an ex-detective, I am more than a little concerned that the Gray woman... that Sr Gray should die so soon after getting me here to look into a suicide which she thought was a murder.'

'Do you think her death is connected to Brinkmeyer's?'

'I don't know. To answer that I would have to know how she died.'

The older man didn't say anything. For moment Jimmy thought he wasn't going to get told anything. It was the younger man who answered.

'She was strangled.'

The older man looked at him, he was annoyed and not doing a good job of hiding it. Who is the real boss here, wondered Jimmy.

'In that case, Inspector, I certainly wouldn't rule out a connection. Has the scene of crime given you anything besides cause of death?'

But the inspector wasn't about to give out any more free information.

'What are your immediate plans, Mr Costello?'

'I don't know.'

'I don't think we would be happy if you were to continue looking into the matter of the student's suicide.'

'Is that a threat?'

'No, Mr Costello, of course not, it is a simple statement of fact. This is a police investigation into a serious crime. Any attempt to involve yourself further in any associated matter might complicate things. If what you have told us is true, and I'm sure it is, but as I've said we'll check, then as an ex-detective I'm quite sure you understand what I mean.'

'Police on the inside, everyone else on the outside? Yes I understand. I'd want it that way as well if it was my case.'

'So, what are your immediate plans?'

'As I'm here I'll take a few more days to get to know the town. So far I've liked what I've seen. Then I'll head back to Rome.'

Jimmy could see that the older one was ready to wrap it up. The younger one he wasn't so sure about. He got the feeling that Inscrutable wanted to take it further.

The older one stood up and the younger one followed suit.

'Thank you for your co-operation, Mr Costello. We'll be in touch if we need to talk further but I doubt that will be necessary. Feel free to leave Vancouver whenever you wish, but if you do wish to leave, please inform us first.'

They headed for the door. At the door Liu looked back.

'I'm glad you like Vancouver, Mr Costello, but to really appreciate it you need more than a few days. At the very least you must spare a day or two to see Chinatown.'

They left and I sat looking at the door.

What the hell did that mean? Liu obviously wasn't a bloke who wasted words, so what was that last bit all about?

Jimmy got up and went across to the window. It was another fine day, sunny and warm. He was getting very fond of this view, he would miss it when he left.

He went to the kitchen area and made himself a cup of tea. So, now what?

See the three people that Gray had lined up then go to Seattle and see what Pa Brinkmeyer had to say? Or should he follow up that Chinatown crack and see if Inscrutable meant anything by it?

No. The pressure was building on this thing and it was all turning nasty. Get out, Jimmy, go through the motions, make enough moves to satisfy McBride, then head for home. Gray had been strangled and that was enough for him. Someone was ready to kill because of this business and it wasn't down to some ordinary villain. Villains didn't strangle people, they shot you or knifed you or beat you to death. They might run a car over you but they didn't strangle you. That was amateur-night stuff, intimate and up close, and that made it too dangerous for him to hang around. You knew where you were with villains, but with amateurs anything could happen, you just couldn't predict what they would do, or sometimes even work out why. No heroics, Jimmy, just go through the motions, go through them very carefully then get out. Do like the man said, leave it to the coppers.

He put his hand to the side of his lower chest. He got a sharp pain there sometimes. The blade must have hit a rib when it went in, nicked it or something. He'd been lucky, he'd lived. Now he was older and wiser. He'd had enough of rough and tumble, he was happy to leave the tough stuff to the tough guys.

He looked at his watch. There was time before he went to see Marvin's friends to walk down to his bar, get a coffee and look out at the water. He'd watch the ferry if it was there and maybe retrieve the hotel's umbrella. He felt better. Now it was all but over he could relax. He didn't need to think about who did what or why and the Church could sort itself out as best it could, stolen art or no stolen art.

But old habits die hard if they ever die at all and, as he got himself ready to go out, his mind wouldn't leave it alone.

Why did the idea of stolen art treasures annoy him? Why couldn't he just forget it? Then he thought of the Gray woman. Strangled, not a nice way to go and a cold way of killing. Yes, he was better out of it. He was too old for this sort of thing any more. McBride should have listened to him. She needed someone younger, someone like that young copper who had been so quiet. He thought about the copper. What was it he had been thinking about during the interview? He put on his jacket. Forget it, leave it alone. Go and have a coffee, watch the boats in the bay and get that bloody umbrella back. Be a tourist and take it easy.

He left the suite and just as he closed the door he heard his phone ringing. He walked on down the corridor. Whatever it was he didn't want to know. He took out his mobile and switched it off and headed for the elevator. He didn't want to know, it was over and he was out of it.

The elevator was empty so Jimmy didn't mind speaking his thoughts out loud.

'Sorry, Philomena, looks like it won't get done after all, at least, not by Jimmy Costello.'

Chapter Seventeen

The taxi couldn't get into the car-park, the entrance and exit both had police tape stretched across them and there was a uniformed policeman standing by each. The taxi pulled away. There were a few cars in the car-park and two police cars. Jimmy's old instincts clicked in. The cars must have been early arrivals who'd parked them as normal. That meant the body hadn't been found then. But there were only five so the discovery must have been made after people started arriving for work but before the rush began, say sixish. So who would be in the chaplaincy building at sixish? One of the uniformed policemen walked to him.

'Can I help you, sir?'

'Is this where it happened, the murder?'

'Who are you, sir?'

'Nobody.'

'In that case would you leave? These buildings are closed until further notice.'

'Sure, officer.'

Jimmy turned and walked along the street headed in the direction the taxi had brought him. Well, he'd turned up, he had made the effort like McBride had wanted. No one else was there. No Sr Gray, no office, no-one to talk to, no meetings. He didn't know the people he was supposed to meet and they didn't know him. Without any way of making contact he could leave...

'Excuse me.'

Jimmy stopped.

She was in her thirties, maybe. It was hard to tell. Short,

black hair, glasses, jacket over a pullover, plain skirt and big feet. Jimmy waited but she stood there waiting for him to speak first.

'Can I help you?'

'You wouldn't be Mr Costello, would you?' Jimmy didn't answer. 'Because if you are, I think Sr Gray wanted me to talk to you. If you're Mr Costello that is.'

Jimmy didn't like her. She spoke as if she was nervous but she didn't look nervous. She looked odd. She wasn't bad-looking or good-looking. She was odd-looking. But, thought Jimmy, if she comes to the chaplaincy she must be…

'I'm Costello.'

She held out a hand.

'I'm Laura, Laura Lawrence. Sr Gray said I should be here to meet you but when I came… well, you saw it. There's a policeman at the door. He told me to go away. What's happened, Mr Costello?'

'Sr Gray has been murdered, strangled. Looks like it happened in the chaplaincy.'

'Oh my God.'

Jimmy waited. News like that usually needed a few minutes. Now he was stuck. He'd broken the news so he couldn't really just walk away and leave her standing on the street.

'Do you still want to talk to me, Miss Lawrence? If you'd like to leave it alone I would understand.'

'What? Yes, I'll talk to you. Sr Gray said it was about Marvin.'

'Yes, about Marvin.'

'Shall we go somewhere?'

'Yes.'

She waited for him to lead.

'Where shall we go?'

'Excuse me?'

'I'm a stranger round here. In fact I'm a stranger in this whole town. Do you know somewhere we can talk?'

'Oh, I see. Yes, there's a place.'

But she didn't move.

'Will we need a taxi?'

'No, it's only a short walk.'

'OK, let's go. Which way?'

She turned back the way he'd just come.

'This way.'

And they set off.

The café wasn't far and wasn't too busy. Jimmy got them coffees and they sat down. He wasn't interested in anything she might say but the sooner he got her talking the sooner he could be on his way.

'Tell me about Marvin.'

'Well, I can't tell you much. I knew him. We were both students at the university.'

'Aren't you a bit old for a student?'

'No. I'm twenty-seven.'

'Isn't that a bit old?'

'Not if you're doing post-doctoral research.'

'I see. Were you and Marvin in the same department? Is that how you met?'

'No, I'm English, he was Art History. We just sort of met. I liked him, he was a very nice guy, easy to talk to.'

'You brought him to the chaplaincy.'

'Yes. He was gay, like me,' she gave him a quick look then continued, 'but he didn't try to hide it.'

'And you do?'

'No, not hide exactly. I'd rather not talk about it if you don't mind. Unless it's important to Marvin's death.'

Jimmy didn't want to talk about it either and he no longer gave a damn about Marvin's death.

'No, it's not important. Was it his idea or yours?'

'Sorry?'

'Going to the chaplaincy, did he ask you or did you suggest it?'

'He sort of asked me.'

'Sort of?'

'He used to go to the university chaplaincy, there was a priest there he spoke to. But he wanted to talk to someone else, someone not connected with the university. I knew about the chaplaincy so I suggested we try there.'

'You used Sr Gray's chaplaincy?'

'No, but I knew about it.'

'Did you know what he wanted to talk about?'

'No, he wouldn't say and I didn't like to pry but he seemed to get what he wanted after he talked to Sr Gray. He must have because he kept on going.'

'And you, did you keep on going?'

'Yes.'

'Why?'

'Why what?'

'Why did you keep on going?'

'Mr Costello, I am not ashamed of who I am or how I am.'

Jimmy waited but she didn't go on.

'Fine, you're not ashamed of how you are. Why did you keep on going to the chaplaincy?'

'I'm not a gregarious person. I have never made friends easily. In fact I have never made friends. I was always a good student and I became satisfied with my studies. I got a good degree and after that there was nothing else I wanted to do so I just kept on studying. Maybe that's all I'll ever do, study. I liked Marvin, he was easy to talk to and he liked to talk, we were almost friends. I went to the chaplaincy because he went. They were nice people there, what you were, well, the way you felt about things didn't come up one way or another. They accepted each other as people.'

'So what did people do at this chaplaincy?'

'We met. Sometimes we'd talk, there were socials, drinks, music. We organised visits, outings, went to the movies. Sr Gray would set up a Mass with a priest every month for those who wanted to go.'

'Are you a Catholic?'

'No, I didn't go to the Masses. I have no interest in religion.'

'Did Marvin?'

'Yes. He was interested.'

'Were you interested in art?'

'No, I know nothing about art, well, only what everyone knows. I'd recognise the *Mona Lisa* if you showed it to me.'

'So what did you talk about?'

'Talk about?'

'Yes. He was interested in art and religion, you weren't interested in either. So what did you talk about?'

She had to think about it.

'Well, I suppose we just talked. We first met when we shared a table for coffee. The place was busy and he asked if he could sit down. I suppose he thought he ought to say something out of politeness so he asked me if I was interested in art.'

'Funny thing to ask a stranger.'

'Oh, he asked that because I'd been to the library and had some books. They were on the medieval period and were open at pages with paintings. He thought they were art books.'

'And they weren't?'

'Well, there was art in them but I was interested in the illuminated texts. That's what I study, medieval manuscripts. I'm doing research on textual…'

'Yes, I'm sure you are. Would you say Marvin was at all suicidal before he killed himself?'

'How would that show itself?'

Good question, how do you spot someone who's about to

top themselves?

'Did his behaviour seem odd or erratic, was he depressed or in some way over-emotional?'

'I don't think so, not when I was with him.'

'Were you with him often?'

'No, not often. We met at the chaplaincy, we went for coffee sometimes. We were both very busy with our studies.'

'Were you surprised when he killed himself?'

'Oh yes, very surprised.'

'And you had no idea why he might have done it?'

'None. May I ask a question, Mr Costello?'

'Sure.'

'Why are you looking into Marvin's death?'

'Sr Gray didn't think it was suicide.'

'But why you? Shouldn't she have gone to the police?'

'She did. They said it was suicide.'

'But how can you...?'

He could see she was trying to find a polite way of asking how come he was sticking his nose in.

'I was a policeman in London. I have a friend who was in the same order as Sr Gray. She asked me to help.'

She seemed relieved, she smiled. It did nothing for her

'And what do you think? Do you think Marvin killed himself?'

'Yes.'

'I see. Now that Sr Gray is...'

'Dead.'

'Yes, what will you do?'

'I'll go home.'

'I see.'

Jimmy stood up. He'd done his duty, he'd stayed and talked to her. If nothing else he could tell McBride he'd interviewed one of Marvin's friends.

'Thanks, Miss...'

The name had slipped his memory.

'Lawrence, Laura Lawrence.'

'Thanks, Miss Lawrence. You've been a great help.'

'Will you want to talk to me again?'

'No, I think you've told me all you can. Goodbye.'

Jimmy left the café and headed back the way they had come, keeping an eye out for a taxi. If he hurried he could get a beer at his bar before taking lunch and be in comfortable time to get out to the airport for his flight to Seattle. He fancied a beer especially after that waste of time. Still, once he'd talked to old man Brinkmeyer he'd have done enough to say he'd tried and that was the point of the thing. Tomorrow he'd sort out McBride's diocesan connection then set off for New York, touch base with the art dealer, then fly back to Rome on the first available flight and he could cobble something together in the way of a report on the journey home.

He saw a taxi, waved it down and gave the name of the bar to the driver. There weren't going to be many more visits to the bar so he didn't want to miss a pint when the opportunity arose. As he looked out of the taxi window his years of police work clicked in again and his mind automatically went over the meeting. He let it, it was something to do. She was a funny woman. Did she seem like a lesbian? But, when you came right down to it, did he have any idea of what a lesbian *would* seem like? Anyway, what was more important was that she knew nothing, so he didn't have to do anything. Nothing to follow up so end of story and time for a pint.

He took out his mobile, thought about switching it on, decided not to and put it away. Why bother? It was almost over. He'd phone from New York to say that he now knew Gray's death had been murder, that she'd been strangled. There was no hurry, like McBride said, she had served her purpose, how she died didn't matter. He looked at his watch again. Thank God the other two he was supposed to talk to hadn't turned up. If he'd had to talk to all three he'd never have got away in time. As it was there was plenty of time for a pint, perhaps even time for two. He smiled to himself, yes, a couple of pints, then something to eat and then off to the airport.

Chapter Eighteen

Brinkmeyer's driver met Jimmy as he came out of Arrivals into the main concourse at Seattle airport. He was a young man in a smart, dark suit and was holding a card with *Mr Costello* on it. Jimmy walked up to him.

'I'm Costello.'

'This way, Mr Costello.'

They walked to the exit doors. Outside, in the drop-off and pick-up area, a large black car was waiting. The driver opened the back door and Jimmy got in. Mr Brinkmeyer, it was hard to think of him as Pa Brinkmeyer now Jimmy was actually face to face with him, matched his car, which was a Bentley. Both were clearly top of the range. Even in shirt, slacks and slip-on shoes he looked like someone who knew the best when he saw it, and when he saw it bought it, though nothing was showy.

The car pulled silently away and joined the airport traffic.

'Thank you for coming, Mr Costello.' Jimmy didn't respond. Brinkmeyer didn't care. 'Why are you looking into the death of my son?'

'I was asked to.'

'By whom?'

'Initially by a friend in London, Sr Philomena McCarthy. She asked me to come across to Vancouver because Sr Gray, who knew your son through her chaplaincy work there, thought he hadn't committed suicide but was murdered.'

'And what do you think?'

Jimmy had come down to do pretty much with Brinkmeyer as he'd done with Laura Lawrence, go through the motions so as to be able to say something to McBride. But now, sitting beside the man, he changed his mind. Brinkmeyer was the kind who could tell a phoney from the real thing so Jimmy decided he might as well be the real thing.

'It doesn't matter what I think. Whatever happened is over as far as I'm concerned. I'll go back to Vancouver and as soon as I can I'll fly out and go home.'

Brinkmeyer sat quietly for a moment.

'You didn't need to fly here to tell me that. You could have told me over the phone.'

'When you phoned I didn't know it was over.'

Brinkmeyer's tone had been friendly at first, then neutral. Now it had a hard edge to it.

'So you came all this way to tell me nothing.'

'If that's the way you want to put it. Personally I don't give a shit, Mr Brinkmeyer. I didn't phone because your wife might have answered, and I assume your wife doesn't know we're meeting and you'd like to keep it that way.'

'I see.'

The tone was back to mild.

'No you don't, but like I said, I don't give a shit one way or the other. He was your son, not mine. If anything needs to be done, you get it done. And like I said, I'll fly out of Vancouver as soon as I can, go back to Rome and forget the whole thing.'

'What's changed since we talked?'

'Sr Gray is dead, murdered. She died sometime last night or early this morning. I don't like the connection. If, and it's a very big if, but if she was killed because of something to do with your son, I don't want to get involved. I didn't mind asking a few questions about a suicide to keep everybody happy but I'm not putting my neck out, not for you, not for anybody.'

They drove on in silence while Brinkmeyer digested

what Jimmy had just told him. It didn't take too long, he was a man who was used to making decisions.

'I won't pretend to understand what's going on, Mr Costello, what it is you are doing, why you are doing it or who you are doing it for. But I would like to know why my son died. You strike me as a man who has some experience in matters like this. Am I right?' Jimmy could see he knew he was right so he didn't bother to lie. He nodded. 'You are or were some sort of policeman, a detective?' Jimmy nodded again. 'Go back to Vancouver and find out why my son died. I'll pay you whatever you ask. I'm a very wealthy man, you may ask for a lot.'

'No thanks.'

'I meant it, whatever you think you should get, double it.'

'I don't need your money. I'm not wealthy like you are but I'm fixed OK. Sorry, Mr Brinkmeyer, I'm out of it. Hire somebody else and give them a lot of money.'

Jimmy was sure Brinkmeyer was a man who usually got what he wanted, but he was also sure it was his money that got it for him. If money wouldn't work Jimmy's guess was that he would be pretty well fucked.

He was right.

When Brinkmeyer spoke he wasn't making any demands or even any offers. He wanted help and he knew he had to ask for it in the right way, humbly and, to give him credit, he made a decent fist of it.

'Why did you come to see me if you're not taking this any further?'

'I told someone I would. Now I have, so I'll be on my way.'

'You have no questions for me?'

'No. Even if I stayed and did what you asked you couldn't help find out what happened. You don't know anything.'

'I knew my son.' Jimmy shrugged. No parent knows their

100

children, the ones who thought they did least of all. 'I didn't understand his choice of sexuality, if it was a choice, but I accepted it. My wife couldn't. She tried to make him see people who said they could help, who told her it was an illness, that he could be cured.' Jimmy said nothing but Brinkmeyer persevered. 'He saw a couple. They did no good, of course, and then he refused to see any more. I'm afraid my wife's attitude and her misguided efforts at help made Marvin go in exactly the opposite direction, he became somewhat promiscuous and made sure my wife knew about it. His mode of dress, behaviour and the friends he brought to the house made life intolerable for my wife. It was an awful time for all of us, I assure you, Mr Costello, a time of true pain and suffering.' Jimmy wasn't interested, if the man wanted to talk he could talk, he wasn't in any big hurry and he'd never been driven around in a Bentley by a chauffeur before. 'Eventually my wife ordered him from the house, disowned him, cut him out of her life.'

Suddenly, and without meaning to, Jimmy surfaced. He'd let his mind wander and a side of him had been listening. He spoke almost before he realised he was saying anything.

'Didn't you get any say? Or is all the money on Mrs Brinkmeyer's side?'

The angry edge came back.

'No, Mr Costello, I'm the one with the money.' Brinkmeyer paused while he got his anger well under control, he knew he still had no leverage in this. 'I made a choice. I didn't think I could hold them together and I also thought Marvin needed to make his own way so I sided with my wife. Marvin left and, without involving my wife, I did what I could for him. I loved my son and I loved my wife. In so far as it was possible I wanted to keep both so I did what I could.'

Jimmy looked out of the window. He was sorry he'd said anything. It was none of his business and he was getting tired of Brinkmeyer and tired of being driven around. When you came down to it a car, even a Bentley, is very much like most other cars.

'You don't know what it's like to lose a son...'

That was it.

'As it happens, I do, and a wife, but that doesn't change anything. People all over the world die for no good reason. Your son's death is not my problem and I'm not about to make it mine.'

'You... you lost your son?'

But Jimmy had had enough. He didn't know Brinkmeyer and he certainly didn't want Brinkmeyer to know anything about him so he changed the subject to the only one Brinkmeyer was interested in.

'Look, just suppose I was to take it further, is there anything you could tell me that might help?'

Brinkmeyer didn't pause. Jimmy could see he'd already thought about it a lot.

'I saw Marvin when I could, which was not often. He seemed happy. I never got any sense that he was emotionally disturbed or in any kind of trouble. If it had been money trouble of any kind he would have contacted me. But the last time I was able to pass through Vancouver was six weeks before he died. Something might have happened in that time. Why did Sr Gray think it was murder?'

Jimmy shrugged. He'd had enough, he'd guessed Brinkmeyer knew nothing and now he had it in his own words to pass on to McBride.

'God knows. Maybe she liked him and didn't want to think he'd kill himself.'

'Could she possibly have been right?'

'He put a shotgun in his mouth and blew half his head off. Does that sound like murder to you?'

'No, Mr Costello, it doesn't sound like murder to me.'

'Me neither. Can we head back to the airport? I'm done

here.'

Brinkmeyer pressed a button.

'Back to the airport, Vincent.'

They sat in silence as the car turned and headed back.

Chapter Nineteen

Jimmy was tired by the time he got back to the Rosedale but overall he was satisfied with the day. He could call McBride and tell her he had nothing to work with, unless the diocesan contact had anything, which he doubted, or the New York art dealer knew something. But the New York dealer didn't worry him because the way he intended to ask the questions the dealer would turn out to know what the others knew - nothing. As he went through the hotel lobby the girl at Reception called to him so he went across.

'You have a message, Mr Costello. Professor McBride phoned and asked you to call her.'

'Thanks.'

Jimmy went to the elevator. On the way up he took out his mobile and switched it on. There were two missed calls, both from McBride.

What the hell, he had gone to the chaplaincy like she asked him to, he had even seen the lesbian. He'd gone down to Seattle and listened to old man Brinkmeyer moan about how tough it all was. He could make his report, that he knew nothing, and make it sound convincing. Tomorrow he would make an appointment with the Crosby character, listen to what he had to say when they met, and then go to New York and see Thurlow Somerset. Then it would be over. There was nothing McBride could do. Why not talk to her?

He called her number.

'Hello, Mr Costello.'

'I've seen the father, he doesn't know anything. He…'

'I'm afraid I have some bad news for you.'

Her voice was like the policeman who had phoned him about Gray. Jimmy knew it wasn't bad news, it was the worst sort of news.

'Go ahead.'

'Sr Philomena is dead.'

She waited a second. She'd guessed he would take it badly. She was right. The elevator stopped, it was Jimmy's floor.

'I'll call you back.'

He walked to his suite, let himself in and went to the kitchen area. He got a glass and picked up the half-size bottle of whisky and filled the glass to the brim. His hands weren't steady and some of the whisky tipped over the edge and ran onto his fingers. He took a long pull which half-emptied the glass, waited a moment, then finished it. He refilled the glass and took another drink. He didn't like whisky and he wasn't used to it. Suddenly he dropped the glass into the sink where it broke. He bent over and vomited on the glass fragments. He stayed bent over until the retching stopped. Then he picked up a tea towel and wiped his mouth. The taste of whisky and vomit filled his mouth and he felt slightly dizzy. He went to a chair, sat down, pulled out his phone and called McBride.

'When?'

'Yesterday.'

'How did it happen?'

'Hit-and-run. She was knocked down three days ago. Since then she'd been in intensive care. Yesterday she died.'

'How come you know?'

'I was told.' Yes, thought Jimmy, you always get told. But only when it's too fucking late. 'There was a letter. It was in her office desk. It wasn't finished but she addressed the envelope. It was for you at the Robson on Rosedale. I asked for a copy to be faxed to me.'

'By whoever told you. Pity they weren't so fucking

thorough in looking out for Philomena.'

'I was not having Sr Philomena watched. I had no reason to suppose she was in any danger.'

'But she still died.'

'Yes, she died. I'm sorry.'

Jimmy didn't care if she was sorry. He cared that Philomena was dead.

'Do you think the hit-and-run was an accident?'

'I have no idea.' Jimmy believed her. She wouldn't play any of her devious games with this. 'Why would anyone want to kill her?'

Jimmy had the answer to that.

'For the same reason someone strangled the Gray woman.'

The phone went silent for a second.

'When?'

'Last night, early this morning.'

'Get out, Mr Costello. Leave tomorrow morning and come back to Rome at once.'

'No.'

'Mr. Costello, three people are dead and they're all connected. We now know Sr Gray was definitely murdered so the death of Marvin Brinkmeyer, whatever the apparent circumstances, may very well turn out to be murder as well.'

'And Philomena?'

'Hit-and-run is not a certain way of killing,' there was a pause, 'but after what you have just told me I think it may well have been deliberate.' She waited but Jimmy said nothing. She knew he was thinking and she was worried by what he might be thinking. 'Get out and come back to Rome. Whatever is going on will be dealt with by others. All you can do on your own is put yourself in danger. This thing is not going at all as I had hoped. There have been developments I had not anticipated.'

As Jimmy listened he realised that she knew something,

something new that she wasn't telling him. That meant the letter.

'What did the letter say?'

'It was about some young woman who had recently come to the refuge. She claimed to know Sr Gray. Here's the bit I think you need to hear.

I didn't like her, there is something wrong about her. But you remember how bad a judge I can be, I thought Janine was such a wonderful girl. Her name is Laura and she is from Vancouver, she is at the university doing some sort of research. But she really does know Sr Gray and she said she knew Marvin Brinkmeyer. In fact I got the impression she is trying to find out what I know. I didn't tell her much but I think she has guessed I know more than I told her. She's been here three days, a willing worker and strong, but I'll be glad when she leaves tomorrow. Maybe it's nothing but please be careful, Jimmy. Remember, young women can be just as dangerous as anybody else. She's late twenties, short black hair, glasses, rather a plain girl. As I say, it is probably me being over-imaginative but as I was the one who got you involved I thought I should...

Is that enough?'

'It's enough.'

'Have you met her, this Laura?'

'Yes, today. She was one of the three that Gray lined up to see me. The police were at the chaplaincy when I went there so I didn't expect to see anybody but she'd made a point of waiting for me. We went for a coffee and talked. I thought I was questioning her but now I think about it she did a pretty good job of questioning me.'

'That settles it. You have to leave.'

'Not yet.'

'Mr Costello, please understand...'

'Get me a meeting as soon as you can with the diocesan bloke.'

'Felton Crosby?'

'Yes. Try to make it tomorrow or the next day at the latest.'

'I think this whole thing has gone beyond any…'

But Jimmy cut off the call and switched off the phone. After a couple of minutes his room phone rang, he ignored it and it stopped. After a few minutes he picked it up and dialled reception.

'How do I get in touch with the police?'

'An enquiry or an emergency?'

'An enquiry.'

Reception explained.

'Thanks.'

He dialled the number he had been given.

'My name is Costello, James Costello. Two officers interviewed me this morning in connection with the murder of a Sr Gray at the chaplaincy attached to St Nicodemus church. Would it be possible to get a message to one of them, a Detective Constable Liu? Yes I'll wait.' When he got a voice he gave it the same message, and once again waited while once again he was transferred. The third voice was more helpful, it could take the message. 'I have no idea if it's important but I have some information which I forgot to give him this morning. It may be nothing but I'd like to tell him anyway. No, I think I'd rather give him the information personally, it's a little complicated. My name is Costello, James Costello, and I'm staying at the Rosedale on Robson. Thank you.'

He put the phone down and went to the kitchen area, and looked at the broken glass and the remains of the vomit in the sink. He pulled some sheets off the kitchen roll and carefully began to collect up the broken glass. He was glad to have something to do. As he collected the shards of broken glass he thought about Philomena and suddenly he found the words of his childhood - and of most of his adult life - automatically coming into his head: *May the souls of the faithful departed, through the mercy of God -*

But there he stopped them. He thought of his wife. She had believed in God, but God hadn't been merciful to her. Jimmy had sat at her hospital bedside while she died of cancer. And their son Michael had believed, believed enough to become a missionary priest. But God had let him die as well, in some God-forsaken part of Africa. And Sanchez, did she believe in God? If she did he hadn't helped her. God hadn't done anything to stop Harry Mercer putting two bullets in her. Now Philomena, who'd given her life to God, was dead.

No, God didn't protect, and God didn't punish. Jimmy dropped the rolled-up parcel of broken glass into the waste basket then rinsed out the sink. Well, if it was too late to protect it wasn't too late to punish, especially as now he knew who it was that should be punished. Laura. Lesbian bloody Laura. She was in the right place for two murders and for Jimmy that was enough, he didn't need any more evidence. It was Laura alright.

He looked at the whiskey bottle standing next to the sink. He didn't like whiskey but there was one more drink in it. He picked up the bottle and poured what was in it into the sink then dropped the bottle into the bin. There was nothing he could do now except wait until the police contacted him. If Liu's crack about Chinatown meant anything the call would come as soon as he got the message, but there was no way of knowing how long that would be. Jimmy looked at his watch, it was nine twenty and he suddenly remembered that he hadn't eaten. But he didn't feel hungry, he felt tired. If Liu got the message it wouldn't be until tomorrow.

He took another glass from the cupboard, filled it with water and washed out his mouth a couple of times to get rid of the taste of the vomit from his mouth, then he went into the bedroom, got undressed and got into bed. Lying in the dark, in the silence of his head, he formed the words he had been unable to finish before. *May the souls of the faithful departed, through the mercy of God, rest in peace.*

Then he said it out loud to the empty bedroom.

'Amen.'

It wasn't much but Philomena would expect it. She would also expect a Mass and some candles. She'd get them. Jimmy let his mind wander, but it didn't wander far.

Who was left to say the prayers for his eternal rest when the time came? Who would light the candles or have a Mass said? The answer was as simple as the question. No one, no one at all.

Chapter Twenty

Jimmy was getting ready to go down to breakfast when the phone rang.

'Costello speaking.'

'This is Detective Liu. I got a message that you had some information for me concerning the death of Sr Lucy Gray.'

'That's right. Are you in your office?'

'Where I am is not your concern, Mr Costello.'

'It's OK to talk?'

'I have contacted you as you asked. If you have information for me I strongly urge you to give it. Obstructing the police, as you are well aware, is a serious offence.'

Liu was doing it by the book, which was just how Jimmy would have done it in his place. He still made one more try.

'Can we meet but keep it unofficial for the time being, keep it just to you and me?'

'I can meet you if you have information material to the case of Sr Gray's death. How I treat our meeting and anything you tell me will depend on what you say when we meet.'

'OK, we'll do it any way you say.'

'I'll be free at eleven fifteen. I'll come to the bar at the Rosedale.'

'Thanks, I'll see you then. I'll wait in the bar.'

Jimmy went down to reception. The young man behind the desk smiled at him.

'Yes, sir?'

'Where's the nearest Catholic church?'

'I don't know but I'm sure I could find out.'

'Thanks. I'm going to have breakfast now. I'll pick up the information when I'm finished.'

'Certainly. Enjoy your breakfast.'

'Thanks.'

Jimmy didn't feel like any breakfast but he ordered coffee so he could sit by himself and think. Philomena's death had changed things. It meant he couldn't leave it alone, now he wanted to get a result and the result he wanted was to nail Laura Lawrence. If she had killed Philomena and Sr Gray it meant that somehow, God knew how, she might have killed Marvin Brinkmeyer. That had to be kept open as a possibility. Another possibility, more likely, was that they were both involved in something and it was so serious that, rather than face the consequences, he'd chosen to kill himself. She, on the other hand, had chosen to kill other people. If the police and a jail sentence were the consequences, Brinkmeyer might have topped himself rather than doing a long stretch. Topping yourself even before you got arrested wasn't unheard of, but it wasn't as common as it happening on remand or while waiting for sentencing. The last possibility, and it was a long shot, was that whatever they were up to was nasty and that his conscience had caught up with him. But it was a very long, long shot.

So, what sort of thing fitted the bill? Drugs would do, and sex might be enough if it was blackmail and the mark was important enough. But from what Gray had told him neither seemed likely. Then again, had she known him that well? Probably not. She only knew the Marvin who came to the chaplaincy, and even then only what he told her. Jimmy dismissed the idea of getting in touch again with the father. He knew nothing.

And then there was Laura Lawrence. She knew Marvin Brinkmeyer, she knew Gray, and she'd pumped Philomena about the suicide and what the Gray woman thought, and as soon as she'd got what she wanted, Philomena got hit by the car. God, she must be an ice-cold bastard, with two killings under her belt and maybe Brinkmeyer as well, she hangs about at the murder scene so she can pump me and see where I fitted in. That must have taken some nerve. But if Laura was the killer and she was tied up with Brinkmeyer in something, where did the chaplaincy come into things? Why did she take Brinkmeyer there in the first place? He didn't see how it could be a cover for them - and if it wasn't a cover and Marvin Brinkmeyer had been serious about the Catholic thing and becoming a priest, then he didn't fit as somebody who was into serious crime, and certainly not someone who was about to kill himself.

Which brought Jimmy back to where he'd started, the possibility that it was murder not suicide. He pushed his cup away. When you found you've gone round in a complete circle it's time to do something different.

He looked at his watch. It was ten past ten. Time to get going, but before he could get up his phone rang.

'Yes.'

'Are you coming back to Rome?'

'No.'

'You know there is nothing I can do to help you there. I can offer you no support of any kind.'

'I know.'

'Would it do any good to talk about this?'

'When I know what this is all about I'll be in touch and you can talk then if you like. Did you get in touch with the bloke at the diocese?'

'Yes, he's expecting your call.'

'There something else I'd like you to do for me.'

'I can't help you, Mr Costello, I've told you my hands are -'

'Get a Mass said for Philomena.'

'I see. Certainly.'

'Thanks.'

Jimmy put his phone away and headed for the reception. There was no one on the desk, so he waited and after a few minutes the young man came out and smiled at him.

'I have what you want, Mr Costello. He reached under the desk and pulled out a street map. He unfolded it and pointed. 'That's us, the Robson, you go along here and turn...'

Jimmy saw that a church had been marked.

'That's fine, I'll sort it out myself. I feel like a walk.'

'Of course.'

Jimmy took the map and folded it so he could see the streets he wanted and left the hotel. He took a look at the map and headed off.

The church, when he arrived, was pretty much the same as most other Catholic churches, a big main altar at the far end from the doors with pillars separating the side aisles from the rows of pews which filled the main body of the place. Jimmy went to one of pillars, where there was a statue and below it the inevitable stand for candles. There were only two women in the church, sitting quietly well away from each other and looking straight at the main altar. The church might have been almost empty, but there were several candles already lit. Always plenty of candles alight in a Catholic church, always people asking for something. Jimmy pulled out his wallet and put a note into the slot of the box below the candles. He picked up a bunch of candles and began to light them one by one. The number of candles didn't matter, nor how much money you put in, what mattered was that you believed. But he didn't believe - at least, he wasn't sure, maybe he did, sometimes. Or maybe that was him hoping he could believe, one day, one day before...

He'd put in a high-denomination note so he took another handful of candles and began to light them. Believing was what mattered, but in the absence of belief use a big bill and plenty of candles. When he was finished he looked up at the sightless eyes of the statue. It was a woman, Our Lady, the Mother of Jesus.

'Now it's your job to look after her. Get it done.'

Jimmy turned away and left the church. He walked back to the hotel, went into the bar and sat down. Liu had played it by the book over the phone and that might be the way he wanted it to stay. But he'd made a point of telling Jimmy not to miss Chinatown, so maybe he'd just wanted it to sound that way if he'd had company when he made the call.

At ten to eleven a man came in with a newspaper, sat down and began to read. At eleven prompt, the shutter of the bar went up and the barman began to do whatever it is bar staff do when they open. Two women came in, one went to the bar and the other sat down. The one at the bar finished ordering and joined her friend. Jimmy waited. After a few minutes the barman came to the women's table with coffee.

At eleven thirty-five Liu walked in and came across to Jimmy's table.

Chapter Twenty-One

Jimmy stood up.

'Thank you for coming, Detective. We can talk here or we could go up to my suite.'

'Come with me, Mr Costello. I'll take us somewhere we can talk.'

'The police station?'

'No.'

'OK, wherever you say, it's your town.'

They left the hotel and got into Liu's car.

'I'm taking you to Chinatown. I told you to make sure to see it, remember?'

'I remember. Was that supposed to mean anything?'

'Did you think it meant anything?'

'I thought it might.'

'Then it might have meant something.'

Was that him being inscrutable again? Jimmy couldn't tell.

'Anywhere special?'

'Just a small bar-restaurant. We could eat or have a drink or just talk.'

'Won't we stick out a bit if we just sit and talk?'

'No. I often go there to just sit and talk.'

'If you say so, it's still your town.'

They drove on in silence until they were in Chinatown. Liu had been right, it was something special. The buildings, except where some modern skyscraper shot up, gave the impression of a chaotic, permanent fun-fair. From the second storey up you could see that the majority looked

Victorian, but at street level it was all brightly coloured shop awnings, electric signs, flags and posters, and everywhere signs in large Chinese characters - spelling out nothing to Jimmy, but obviously much more than mere decoration. Above the streets, along them and across them, power-lines criss-crossed the roadways. It was as if the whole place had been run up in a hurry and had become a fixture by accident more than design. But despite the impression it all gave to Jimmy of something from a film or a stage set he could see that no one here was playing at being Chinese. It might be a big pull with the tourists but that didn't stop it being the real thing.

The traffic moved slowly through the crowded, bustling main streets and eventually Liu turned the car into one of the many even more crowded side streets, where pedestrians seemed to have right of way by sheer force of numbers. He drove even more slowly and finally pulled in outside a small bar-restaurant.

'This is it.'

'Can you just park here?'

But Liu ignored the question and got out so Jimmy followed. He noticed Liu hadn't bothered to lock the car. Either he was very careless or very confident.

On one side of the restaurant entrance there were about eight tables where people were already sitting and eating. On the other side was a bar with about the same number of tables, where people were talking and drinking. It wasn't full but it was quite busy. Jimmy noticed that all of the customers were Oriental and the voices he heard weren't speaking English.

Liu turned to him.

'Eat, drink or just talk?'

'Eat. I didn't have any breakfast and I could do with something now.'

Liu went across to a table in the dining side and they sat

down. Out of nowhere a waitress was suddenly by their side. She had a big smile on her face and said something in Chinese to Liu. Liu smiled back and answered in Chinese, then looked at Jimmy.

'Do you want to see a menu?'

'Are you eating?'

'Yes.'

'I'll have whatever you're having.'

'Fine.'

Liu rattled off something to the waitress who made some marks on her pad and went away.

'They know you here?'

'They know me. So, Mr Costello, down to business.'

Jimmy looked around; there was no way some of what they would say wouldn't be overheard.

'I thought we were going somewhere we could talk.'

'We're there. No one will listen-in, I assure you.'

'Oh well, as long as you assure me.'

'My great-uncle owns this place. The waitress is a sort of cousin. I know most of these people and they know me. I've used it plenty of times and believe me, there's never been a problem. What is it you want to tell me?'

'Are we off the record?'

'Not yet. I'll decide that when I've heard what you've got to say. But I'm on my own, there's nobody else official to hear what you've got to tell me. Settle for that for the time being.'

Jimmy decided he would, what choice did he have?

'A couple of things have happened that are connected with Sr Gray's death. First, I went to the chaplaincy office to a meeting Sr Gray had set up with three people who knew Marvin Brinkmeyer. Naturally I couldn't get in, so I was giving up and leaving when a young woman introduced herself, Laura Lawrence. She was one of those I was supposed to meet.'

'So?'

'The same Laura Lawrence was in London recently and stayed for a few days at the refuge run by Sr Philomena McCarthy. Have you checked my story with Sr McCarthy yet?'

'Not yet.'

'Then don't bother. She was the victim of a hit-and-run three days ago and last night I got told that she had died in hospital. You can check with the Met, but my guess is they have no line on who was driving the car.'

'Why do you think that?'

'Because I think the young woman who met me at the chaplaincy and was staying at the refuge three days ago killed Philomena and she's back here, large as life and free as a bird.'

'I see.'

'I hope you do. This Lawrence woman knew them both and was in the right place for when Gray got strangled and Philomena got hit.'

'How did you know about London?'

'Philomena wrote me a letter. In it she said a young woman had turned up at the refuge, Laura Lawrence. Lawrence said she knew Sr Gray so Philomena let her stay at the refuge for a time and help out. While Lawrence was there she tried to find out what Sr Gray had told Philomena about Marvin Brinkmeyer's suicide. Philomena felt there was something not right about Lawrence, she didn't know what it was but it worried her. Lawrence was due to come back to Vancouver and Philomena told me to be careful. She was obviously worried about this Lawrence woman and as it turned out she was right, only she was the one who needed to be careful.'

'When did you get this letter?'

Jimmy hadn't had time to work out a watertight explanation so he did the best he could.

'I didn't. A friend of mine in Rome picked it up from my apartment, opened it and got in touch - and before you ask, it was Professor McBride, the one who was at the Dublin conference with Philomena and Gray. She picks things up for me when I'm away.'

'And opens your mail?'

'Yes. I never get anything personal, not until this letter from Philomena.'

'This doesn't help your story about how you got involved. Two of the people who can confirm what you have told us have died. One has been murdered and another, if your hit-and-run is true, has been killed under suspicious circumstances.'

'Sod confirming my story. What I'm saying is -'

The waitress came, put cutlery and napkins on the table and waited.

'Anything to drink, Mr Costello?'

'Is it going to be hot, spicy hot?'

'Not particularly, it's steak and French fries.'

Jimmy felt relieved. He had been getting too worked up, trying to get Liu on his side too soon. The waitress had come at the right time, and the news that the lunch was steak rather than something that would scorch his throat was a bonus.

'Yes, a beer would be nice.'

'Any special kind?'

'Just what comes to hand.'

Liu said something to the waitress who left.

'Doesn't she speak English?'

'She's learning. She only came over from Hong Kong six months ago.' Liu busied himself unfolding his napkin so Jimmy followed suit. The waitress returned with their steak and chips, smiled again at both of them, then said something in Chinese and left. Liu picked up his knife and fork and started cutting into his steak. 'Keep going. Your beer's on its way.'

Jimmy started on his meal. It was a good steak.

'Before I go on I should tell you what I want.'

'OK, tell me. I don't mind you telling me so long as you understand you probably won't get it.'

The waitress arrived again with two bottles of beer and two glasses. Once she was gone Jimmy began.

'Philomena was a friend, a very good friend. She wanted me to come and look into Brinkmeyer's suicide as a favour to her. Now it turns out that Brinkmeyer's death has given me the only lead I have to whoever killed Philomena, this Laura Lawrence. I want to find her.'

'And do what?'

'Put her in court on a charge of murder and be sure there's a cast iron case to get a conviction. What did you think I'd want to do?'

Liu didn't look up from his steak which was disappearing fast.

'I don't know, that's why I asked.'

Jimmy felt a twinge of annoyance.

'Look, from what I've told you, you have a suspect, a woman who was in the right place for both killings, Laura Lawrence. She was connected to both victims and had opportunity both times.'

Liu cleared up his last few French fries, put down his knife and fork, pushed his plate away and poured himself some beer.

'And the motive would be?'

Jimmy was rapidly losing interest in his meal. Getting Liu on board was taking all his attention and effort. He took one last mouthful of steak and then pushed his plate away.

'The motive has to be something to do with Marvin Brinkmeyer's death.'

'Are you going to leave that?'

'Yes, somehow talking to you has taken away my

appetite.'

Liu pushed his plate to one side, reached over and pulled Jimmy's plate in front of him. He picked up his knife and fork and cut a piece of the steak.

'It would be an insult to the cook to send any steak back.'

'And we don't want to do that, do we? We have two murders to talk about but we don't want to insult the cook.'

'That's right, he's a sort of cousin.'

Jimmy gave up. He poured himself some beer, took a drink and waited until Liu had cleared the plate and pushed it away. From nowhere the waitress was at the table again, smiling and clearing away the two empty plates. Liu rattled off something in Chinese. The waitress looked at Jimmy, giggled then left.

Liu poured some more beer.

'Will this Professor of yours back up everything you've told me?'

'Yes.'

'And can anyone vouch for her?'

'The Pope and a dozen Cardinals.' That got home, thought Jimmy, as a flicker of surprise passed across Liu's face. 'She's well known in Vatican circles and among the academic community of Rome. If anyone has to do any vouching it will be you.'

'OK, it seems you can back up your story as to why you're here, so what do you want from me?'

'I told you, I want this Laura Lawrence character, I want to nail her. I can't do it alone, I need help.'

'What sort of help?'

'With what I've given you there should be enough for you to look at the Brinkmeyer suicide again, and when you do you can ask questions. I need to be told what the answers are.'

Liu took a drink of beer. So did Jimmy. It wasn't very good.

'Even if I pass on what you've given me, I won't be the one who gets to look at the suicide again. That will be someone else. I'm on the Gray case.'

'Maybe, but the way I look at it Laura Lawrence connects Philomena, Sr Gray and Marvin Brinkmeyer, so Philomena's death and Brinkmeyer's suicide become legitimate avenues of enquiry in the Gray case. I don't see any problem with you asking the questions I need.' Liu didn't respond. 'At the very least you'll need to find Lawrence and talk to her.'

Liu finished his beer.

'I'll think about it.'

Jimmy knew that was the best he was going to get. He picked up his glass, looked at it and put it down. It was fairly tasteless and gassy. He wouldn't finish it.

'Do you want to finish my beer? If the barman is a sort of cousin of yours I wouldn't want him offended.'

Liu stood up. Their talk was over.

'Come on, I'll take you back to your hotel.'

They drove back to the hotel in silence, both had plenty to think about.

At the hotel Jimmy got out and as he was about to close the car door Liu finally spoke.

'If I get anything I'll be in touch.'

'Fair enough. Thanks for the meal.'

'That's OK, it's on expenses. It was business. This is still official, I log everything and it stays that way until I say otherwise. If I ever do.'

Jimmy closed the door. Liu pulled away and Jimmy went into the hotel. Suddenly he felt very tired, even though it was only early afternoon. He went up to his suite and as he opened the door the phone began ringing. He ignored it, he was too tired. Too much had happened and it had all happened too quickly. What he needed now was rest. The phone stopped ringing.

Maybe it was the bloke from the Diocese, the one who was expecting his call. Or McBride. Or one of Liu's sort of cousins. Or God almighty. He didn't care. He went into the bedroom and kicked off his shoes then fell onto the bed. The phone began ringing again. He let it ring. He would see to it later. Right now all he wanted to do was sleep.

Chapter Twenty-Two

Inspector Brownlow had phoned at ten and they arrived at eleven fifteen but, as the interview was taking place in his suite, not at the police station, Jimmy still felt ahead of the game. It was the senior officer, Brownlow, who was doing the talking again. Liu was busy practising his Madame Tussaud's impression, still and silent.

'Detective Liu has told me about your information. Tell me, Mr Costello, was there any reason why you made your message personal for Detective Liu? Why not me?'

'I could remember his name. I'd forgotten yours.'

'Can I see this letter? The one from your friend who died.'

'No.'

'No?'

'It's in Rome. A friend has a key to my apartment, Professor McBride. She collects my mail. I told her to call me if any of it was important. She phoned me and told me about the letter from England.'

'You didn't mind her reading your mail?'

'No, I get very little mail and most of what I get is bills or junk. I can't remember the last time I got anything personal. If you want to see the letter I can get Professor McBride to fax it to you.'

'Thank you, Mr Costello, that would be most helpful.'

'Shall I get it faxed here to the hotel and bring it to you or do you want it sent to the station?'

'Here will do. You say this Laura Lawrence was waiting for you when you went to the chaplaincy?'

'Yes. She was one of the three Sr Gray had arranged for me to meet. I told you about the meeting when you came the first time, remember?'

'Yes, I remember. Why do you suppose she waited for you?'

'At the time I thought she just wanted to know what was going on. Now I think she wanted to see what I knew and what, if anything, I was going to do. I'm afraid I was sloppy and she did better at asking the questions than I did. Still, that may have been a break for me.'

'A break?'

'If she was the one who killed Sr Gray and Sr Philomena and thought I knew anything or was going to poke around too much I might be in the morgue now, not here chatting with you two.'

'Really, Mr Costello, do you want us to think that this Laura Lawrence is some sort of homicidal maniac? I assure you, pre-meditated, multiple murders are very rare, and one where the victims are separated by six thousand miles would probably be unique. As an ex-detective I would have thought you'd know that.'

'Yes, they are rare. But I still think you may have just found one in your back yard. I think Lawrence has killed twice, and if Brinkmeyer's death was somehow down to her and not suicide, it would be three times. I don't get the feeling that one more dead body would have worried her. As it is, she thinks I'm harmless.'

'Harmless?'

'When I spoke to her I was ready to pack it in and go home. She could see I wasn't interested in doing anything.'

'But now you want to stay on and find out what really happened?'

'Now I have information which I didn't have then. So do you. Things have changed.'

The inspector stood up. Liu followed suit.

'Let us know when you have that fax and we'll collect it. And the name's Brownlow, Inspector Brownlow. Try to remember it this time, Mr Costello. If you have any further information please make sure you contact me. Good day.'

They left. Nobody shook hands and nobody said goodbye. The inspector had been polite but Jimmy could see it had been a strain. Liu must have taken a shed-load of flak when he told Brownlow about the meeting.

It was now twenty to twelve and Jimmy wanted to be on time at the church, so he left his suite a few minutes after the detectives. He'd phoned the priest, who had agreed to say the midday Mass for Philomena. Outside it was raining again and he hadn't got round to buying a raincoat, but neither had he picked up the hotel umbrella from the waterfront bar so he didn't like to go back in and ask for another. The rain wasn't heavy so he kept on going.

It took just over ten minutes to get to the church and once inside he walked over to where candles burnt in front of a statue of Our Lady. He put some coins into the box and picked out three candles. He lit them one at a time, one for Bernie, one for Michael, and one for Philomena. He looked up at the blind eyes of the statue.

'I'm sorry if I was short the other day. I have a lot on my mind and Philomena's death sort of got in amongst me. Look after them all... please.' Then he let the old formula form into words. 'May the souls of the faithful departed, through the mercy of God, rest in peace. Amen.'

He went and sat down in a nearby pew. There were about thirty people scattered about the big church. He thought of Philomena. 'Rest in peace...' - she had never been a great one for resting. She hated any kind of idleness and now here he was asking Our Lady to pray that she should spend her eternity in permanent rest. He tried again for another prayer.

'Eternal rest grant unto them, O Lord, and let perpetual light shine upon them. May they rest in peace. Amen.'

Another formula learned from his mother as a child and uttered automatically how many thousands of times? It was no better. An eternity of rest, the peace of inaction. Was that really what he wanted God to give to his wife, his son, and to Philomena? Some sort of never-ending, supernatural sun-bathing in the brightness of God's presence? He had been a Catholic all his life, he still was in a way, but he had never heard that there was anything else on offer after death, just eternal rest and the eternal presence of God which somehow got translated into peace. It didn't sound so very different from the only other alternative he could imagine, oblivion. In fact it sounded almost exactly the bloody same, except that oblivion seemed the better choice. At least that way it was all over, finished.

A bell rang. Jimmy left his thoughts and stood up with the others as the priest came out to the altar and the Mass began.

As another old formula, known since childhood, began to unfold, he decided it didn't matter what he believed or didn't believe. He wasn't doing this for himself, he was doing it for people who had believed, had died believing. It wasn't faith, it was duty, or perhaps not even duty but a debt, a debt that had to be paid even if he half-believed that the currency of payment was worthless.

After the Mass he went into the sacristy, thanked the priest and gave him an envelope with the Mass offering in it. The priest took it and that was that. Jimmy left the church and headed down to the bay. Time for a pint and lunch, then he would go and see the bloke from the Diocese. Mr Crosby had phoned him at nine and said Professor McBride had been in touch and asked him to set up a meeting. He could see Jimmy at three if that was convenient. It was. If McBride was right then this was the bloke who would tell him how the whole thing had got started.

Chapter Twenty-Three

Felton Crosby was a dapper little man in his mid-fifties with an office in a building near the Cathedral.

'Professor McBride made it sound urgent that I talk to you so I rearranged today's schedule, but I'm afraid I have a meeting which I must attend in half an hour. What can I do for you, Mr Costello?'

'Did you know a young art history student called Marvin Brinkmeyer?'

'No, I didn't know him. I met him, once, in this office.'

'What was the meeting about?'

'Some paintings he said he was interested in.'

'What paintings and what was his interest?'

'He wouldn't say.'

'He wanted to talk about some paintings but he wouldn't say which ones?'

'Yes, I didn't understand it either. He seemed a genuine young man, not any type of crank. He was polite but quite insistent. He said the Diocese was in possession of stolen art, paintings which were of great value. He wanted to talk to someone in authority.'

'Did he explain what it was he wanted done about this stolen art?'

'No. As I said, he was polite and seemed, well, normal, but he was very insistent.'

'Insistent about what? I must say, Mr Crosby, I'm finding it hard to follow what it was Marvin Brinkmeyer wanted from you.'

'Yes, I found it difficult myself. The best I can do is to

say that he seemed to believe that if the diocese found that he had uncovered this stolen art, the matter might be covered up somehow.' How right he was, thought Jimmy. That was exactly what McBride wanted. 'I told him I couldn't help. I assured him that the diocese possessed no stolen art, valuable or otherwise.'

'And what did he say?'

'He said he could accept that the diocese may have come into possession of the pictures in good faith but that did not change the fact that they were stolen. He urged me to arrange a meeting with someone in authority. Really, Mr Costello, I almost believed he was telling the truth. He seemed very genuine and quite sure of what he was saying. He was most convincing.'

'You believed him?'

'No. Mr. Costello. The diocese has no stolen paintings. He obviously thought what he was saying was true but as it happens we have no paintings at all of any real value - not commercial value, that is.'

'How can you be so sure he was wrong?'

'Because I handle the insurance, Mr Costello. I have an inventory of all diocesan artefacts that require insurance and that includes paintings. I am responsible, among other things, for seeing that the inventory is kept up to date and regularly re-valued, and insurance premiums adjusted accordingly. This diocese is not like some European ones. We have inherited no Old Masters, we are not the custodians of any great works of art. The art we have is religious art, predominantly from the nineteenth century onwards. Art of that sort has no significant commercial value unless painted by an established and collected artist. To the modern eye and viewed solely in terms of artistic value, most of the paintings the diocese possesses would, I suppose, be classed as bad art. They are devotional works, of interest and value only to the faithful. Our most valuable painting is probably worth no more than several thousand dollars on the open market. Worth insuring, certainly, but by today's standards not of any great value.'

Crosby sounded very sure of what he was saying and none of it was helpful.

'He said paintings, more than one, several?'

'Yes, paintings, and I got the impression it was several.'

'He gave you no idea of where they were?'

'No.'

'What did you tell him?'

'That I would look into the matter but that I was almost one hundred per cent sure there was no basis to his claim.'

'And he accepted that?'

'No. He said he would give me a week to change my mind and to set up a meeting with someone of sufficient authority to deal with the matter.'

'Just as a matter of interest, who would that have been?'

Crosby had to think about that.

'The bishop, I suppose, or possibly the vicar general. I really don't know.'

'And what happened a week later?'

'Nothing. I never saw the young man again. I suppose he gave up when he realised he would get nowhere. I have no idea what he was up to.'

'Do you know what happened to him?'

'No.'

'He committed suicide.'

Crosby paled visibly.

'Oh my God.'

'When did your meeting with him take place?'

Jimmy's news had obviously shaken him. 'It wasn't anything to do with why he came to see me, was it?'

'I don't know. I'm trying to find out. When did your meeting take place?'

'He seemed such a nice young man, other than the

131

business about the paintings. He didn't give any impression of someone suicidal.'

'What impression do suicides usually give, in your experience?'

'Oh yes, I see what you mean. What I meant was, he didn't seem to me…'

'When did your meeting take place?'

'Yes, of course, sorry, your news gave me a shock. One hears about these things but when it is someone…'

'Your meeting, Mr Crosby.'

'Yes, the meeting.'

He opened a desk diary and went back through the pages.

'July the fifteenth at eleven o'clock.'

The suicide had happened on the following Friday. If there was stolen art, and according to McBride there could be, Laura Lawrence was involved in it. She could have found out about the meeting with Crosby and, bingo, Marvin conveniently agrees to blow his head off. Jimmy wondered how she managed to get him to do it.

'Could it be like Brinkmeyer said, is there any way someone could hide stolen art somewhere in the diocese without you or anyone else knowing?'

'How, Mr Costello?' A thought occurred to him. 'And perhaps more importantly, why? Why steal it if you're going to give it to the Church?'

It was a bloody good question. Jimmy wished he'd thought of it. He was supposed to be the detective.

'Yes. A good question, Mr Crosby. Did Brinkmeyer tell you anything about the paintings - size, subject matter, anything about where they had been stolen from?'

'Yes. He said the paintings had been stolen during the war.'

'He definitely said stolen in the war?'

'Yes, I'm sure.'

'Which war?'

'Oh, I'm afraid I don't know, I didn't ask. I just assumed the Second World War.'

As it happened, Jimmy assumed that as well. But if that was the case then why had the stuff surfaced only now?

'Things like that, valuable stuff that disappeared during the war, would eventually re-surface and get back into the legitimate market, wouldn't it?'

'Perhaps, I couldn't say. I know very little about the art world.'

'But it is possible?'

'I suppose so, but the war was a long time ago. If someone had hidden them, surely they would have retrieved them and sold them some years ago. Anyone who might have been involved would be a very great age by now, probably dead.'

Yes, thought Jimmy. I'd got that far myself.

'Say somebody gave them to the diocese, no, say somebody loaned them. That way they could be looked after until they were retrieved. Would that be possible?'

'No, because as far as I know the diocese has no art on loan, valuable or otherwise. Mr Costello, I deeply regret that the young man took his own life, but I don't see how his story could make any sense, how I might have been any help.'

No, thought Jimmy, he couldn't make any sense of it either.

According to Brinkmeyer's story there were several valuable stolen paintings sitting somewhere in the diocese. But if he'd found that out, why had no one else noticed, especially if it was art valuable enough to steal in the first place and now to kill for? Another piece of information suddenly clicked into place. If the Lawrence woman had indeed killed for it, that meant she'd found some way of getting her hands on it. But where was it?

The interview had gone about as far as it could but

Jimmy had one last question to ask.

'Who did you tell about this meeting?'

'Well, I don't honestly don't think I told anyone, it all seemed so bizarre. No, wait a minute... I phoned the insurance company we use. I told someone there.'

'Why did you do that?'

'One has to be careful, Mr Costello. I told the insurance company what had happened and asked if I should do anything.'

'And what did they advise?'

'They said do nothing unless he came back. If he did, then go to the police and let them deal with it.'

Jimmy stood up, he wasn't going to get any more here.

'Thank you for your time, Mr Crosby. I can't say you've been helpful but I appreciate your time.'

'There is nothing to it, is there, Mr Costello? There can't be.'

'No, there's nothing to it. Brinkmeyer must have killed himself for some other reason, or maybe for no reason at all. He couldn't have been completely rational if he came here accusing the diocese of hoarding wartime loot, could he? I suspect he did it while the balance of his mind was disturbed. The police think so too. Sad, but unfortunately not all that uncommon.'

'A tragedy though, a young life wasted like that.'

'Yes, a tragic waste. Thanks once again. I don't think it's likely but if you do think of anything that might help I'm at the Rosedale on Robson. I'll see myself out.'

Chapter Twenty-Four

It had begun to rain again so once Jimmy was outside the diocesan offices he went into the first bar he came to and ordered a beer. When it came it was cold, almost tasteless lager. So, Vancouver wasn't perfect after all.

He took it to a table and went over the interview. Laura Lawrence was in on whatever it was before Marvin Brinkmeyer went to the diocese, and she killed him or got him to kill himself after he'd visited Crosby. The boy was making waves about the stolen art so he got stopped. Did he tell Lawrence he was trying to get the diocese involved, or was it possible that someone in the insurance company had told her? It was possible, but highly unlikely. Brinkmeyer trying to blow the whistle to the diocese gave Lawrence a motive. Fine. But he still had no lead at all on the art itself. He was looking for stolen pictures which were valuable enough for three people to have been killed. Where was it? Brinkmeyer said in the diocese and Crosby said no way.

Jimmy tried his drink again but it was no better. When you came right down to it, what had he actually got? A killing which looked more like a suicide than most suicides do, a strangled nun, and another nun knocked down and killed six thousand miles away. And all connected to some mysterious stolen paintings.

But was it connected?

Maybe it was no more than wishful thinking on his part. He wanted it all to be connected because he needed it that way to pin Philomena's murder on…

No, not only because he wanted it. McBride also said so,

and McBride had told him to get out because she thought he might get killed. She believed in the connection.

He took out his mobile and dialled.

'Yes, Mr Costello?'

She *did* live in that damned office.

'How did you know about it? How did you get told about the paintings?'

'It started with a letter.'

'What letter?'

'A letter was sent to the diocese by the art dealer friend of Marvin Brinkmeyer. He said that the diocese was in possession of paintings looted during the war. They didn't know the paintings were in their possession but nonetheless, that was the case. The paintings had been covered with new canvas, and new pictures painted to hide the originals. He was prepared to say where these paintings were on one condition. That he be given first refusal of the canvases that had been used to cover the originals. If the diocese refused his terms he would go to the media.'

'Why the hell didn't you just tell me this at the beginning?'

'Because Marvin Brinkmeyer committed suicide and the art dealer has disappeared. He went missing the week after Brinkmeyer's death.'

'Dead?'

'Up until Sr Gray's murder I couldn't be sure. But I think it's safe, since three others involved are dead, to assume that Thurlow Somerset is also dead. As for not telling you, I don't see that anything has changed. If you had gone to New York you would have found out that he was missing and had been since shortly after Brinkmeyer's suicide. Once you had that information you would have known everything I know.'

She always had an answer. Not exactly the right answer, but she always had one.

'So we have nothing. No one knows where these

paintings are and all the people who could help are dead.'

'Marvin Brinkmeyer's suicide was our only way into this. You will have to work it out for yourself, if you still insist on going on with the matter. I strongly advise you to come back to Rome. If you do I will see that the police are informed and then it will become their business to find the paintings, if they can and if they want to.'

'And if the media get hold of it, which, if the police get involved, they will?'

'The Church has weathered worse and will again. It is not worth getting you killed.'

'I know. It would be such a nuisance to have to replace me.'

She said nothing so he hung up.

A tricky bastard, McBride, he thought. But clever, you couldn't deny that. Well, as usual she had got what she wanted. Jimmy looked out of the bar's window. Umbrellas were coming down, so Jimmy pushed away his lager and left the bar. Time to get going again. He wanted to think and walking helped, so as the rain had stopped, he began to walk.

Through the wood, through the wood, but never touch a bit of the wood. What is it? A penny in a man's pocket.

It had been a silly riddle his dad had told him as a child and somehow the words had stuck. In the diocese, in the diocese but not in any part of the diocese. Where is it? Whose pocket were those paintings in?

Marvin Brinkmeyer could see it and Thurlow Somerset could see it, but it wasn't anywhere other people would see it. The paintings had been covered over with other paintings and Somerset wanted first refusal of the ones doing the covering. But surely no one covers valuable stolen art with other bits of important art. Or do they?

But the diocese had no important art.

Christ, it was like a bloody blank jigsaw puzzle. How

could you know which bit went where? Where were there several pictures on display that got a student and an art dealer interested enough to give them a very close look, such a close look that they found they were covering some really valuable art?

It was a riddle alright, but not the simple little one his dad had liked. He'd been a bus driver and said that driving a bus in central London was like a riddle. It was a riddle how any of them ever got where they were going.

In his mind he was a child again and they were all sitting round the table in the kitchen, the meal was over and they were talking. Mum was at the sink doing the washing up and his dad made the joke about London buses being a riddle. Mum had said, 'That's not a riddle it's a mystery. We're not meant to understand Central London traffic, it's like the blessed Trinity, a divine mystery.'

And they all laughed.

Mum was the clever one. Even as a young child he sensed it from the way she talked. She should have had an education, been a teacher or something. As it was she was a housewife married to a bus driver. She'd always seemed happy, but now Jimmy wondered. Was it like Bernie, all an act for the sake of the husband and kids? Never let them see you crying?

He brushed the scene from his mind. The past was the past: you couldn't change it and you couldn't forget it, but you could leave it alone. If you did that, maybe it might leave you alone. So he thought of something else.

As far as he could see, the only way he could make any progress was for Liu to come on board. But he put that down as fifty-fifty at best, especially if Brownlow had come the heavy about the whole thing. It would probably depend on what, if anything, they got when they took a second look at the suicide. If they took a second look. The clouds looked threatening and Jimmy could see that the rain would soon start again. He'd have to buy that bloody mac, or an umbrella. He looked among the traffic for a taxi, get one before the rain comes and everyone wants one. He spotted one and flagged it down. He'd get back to the Rosedale and maybe take a kip. There was nothing he could do at the moment so that's what he'd do. Nothing.

Chapter Twenty-Five

Liu took three days to get in touch. Jimmy didn't mind, he knew it would take time so he became a tourist. He went on the ferry to North Vancouver. The hotel told him Victoria Island was worth a visit so he went, but he didn't like it. It reminded him too much of England, but an England that was cleaner and with better manners. He took in the quaintness of Gas Town and explored the bars and the restaurants. He drank good beer and watched the world go by. The weather had turned kind: no rain, sunny and warm. He didn't let himself think about killings or stolen art. If Liu came through there would be plenty of that to come.

Liu phoned in the early evening of the third day of waiting and gave him the name and address of the place in Chinatown where they'd met.

'Take a taxi and be there at eleven thirty tonight.'

Jimmy found Liu sitting at the same table. This time Liu didn't ask him if he wanted to eat and Liu's cousin brought no drinks. It wasn't far off midnight but the place, like everywhere else in Chinatown, was lit up and busy and looked like staying busy. The place didn't seem to have heard about going to bed.

'You finished for the day?'

Liu shook his head.

'No.'

'You work late hours.'

'Didn't you?'

'I suppose so. It's a long time ago.'

Liu got down to business.

'Brownlow doesn't want you anywhere near his case.'

'You dragged me all the way over here at this time of night to tell me that?'

'No, I dragged you over here to tell you what we got about the suicide.'

Did that mean he was on board?

'OK, what have you got?'

'Nothing.'

'Nothing?'

'It wasn't investigated, not properly. Someone puts a shotgun in their mouth and their thumbprint is on the trigger. What's to investigate?'

'But you don't like it?'

'I don't like sloppy police work.'

'Tell me about it.'

'It happened in the university grounds, late afternoon. He sat on a bench in a secluded place, put the gun in his mouth and shot himself. A couple of students heard the shot, went to see what it was and found him.'

'How long between them hearing the shot and getting to the body?'

'Not long. They weren't far away.'

'I thought you said it was a secluded spot?'

'That's why they weren't far away. They wanted privacy too.'

'I see. Did they see anybody?'

'No.'

'What was there other than the gun?'

'Nothing. Just the body and the gun.'

Jimmy was disappointed. He'd hoped for more. 'I see.'

'Doesn't that strike you as odd?'

'Odd?'

'Yes. How did he get to the bench carrying a shotgun and nobody noticed anything?'

Damn, another question he should have been asking.

'It was a secluded part of the university.'

Liu ignored Jimmy's response and Jimmy agreed with him.

'He still had to get there from his room or wherever. A student walking around with a shotgun over his arm and nobody notices?'

'Under his coat?'

'He was wearing a light sports jacket. He had it on when he pulled the trigger. Who puts their jacket back on before they blow their brains out?'

'And nobody asked the question?'

'Like I said, it wasn't properly investigated. It must have been the same with you sometimes. You don't have the time or the manpower so you take what's on offer. It looks like suicide so it's suicide. If it looks like a duck, walks like a duck and quacks like a duck...'

'It's a duck. But even if the police decided it was suicide from the word go, the question of how the gun got there had to be asked?'

'It was, but not properly answered. Brinkmeyer got the gun there somehow, maybe like you said, under his jacket. How didn't matter. What he did with it when he got there, that mattered.'

'But now you think the how matters?'

'Now it matters.'

'To you or to Brownlow?'

'It matters to Brownlow. But like I said, you're a civilian, he doesn't want you near any police investigation.'

'I gave you the information you needed to take a second look at the suicide. Doesn't that get me some of the way in?'

'No. It puts you further out. If he lets you help he won't get all the credit, but if you cause problems he'll definitely get all the blame. You see, Brownlow has a problem. He thinks he deserves promotion so he wants results, but he doesn't want to point the finger at any of his colleagues and say "screw-up" where the suicide is concerned. That isn't the way people get to climb the ladder. As far as he's concerned it will stay suicide and no further questions will get asked. Not officially anyway.'

'And unofficially?'

'You were a detective, you know how these things work. He wants a result in the Gray case to help his promotion, but he's still a good officer. If, on my own initiative, I ask questions, he'll listen to the answers, but my questions have to be connected to the investigation in hand, the Gray killing. We know that Brinkmeyer was linked to Sr Gray through the chaplaincy. We followed up the faxed copy of the letter you gave us and checked with your Professor McBride who, like you said, is a very highly rated lady with impeccable friends and absolutely above any suspicion. She confirmed that Gray had told both her and your London nun Sr McCarthy she thought Brinkmeyer hadn't killed himself, which was why you got called in to come and poke your nose around. Gray dies and your nun dies. That means we now know all three deaths have something else in common.'

'They were all linked to Laura Lawrence.'

'Yes.'

'I don't see how, but I think Lawrence engineered Brinkmeyer's death.'

'Look, get this into your head: all Brownlow wants is a result in the Gray killing. If anything you bring helps in that, fine. If not then forget it.'

Jimmy wasn't sure what to do. He could add Thurlow Somerset's disappearance to the body count but that would give them the stolen art. He wasn't ready to do that yet. He tried to edge a bit further.

'Anything concerning Laura Lawrence, including the suicide and the London hit-and-run, should help. She's your best bet for the killer. Anyone of her description seen near the suicide?'

'No one asked. They had the two who found the body and when they told their story as far as the police were concerned that was that.' Liu paused, he knew Jimmy wasn't going to like what he was about to tell him. 'I checked though, I tried to find out where Lawrence was at the time of Brinkmeyer's death.'

'And?'

'And there is no one at the university among staff or students called Laura Lawrence. I checked with two or three people who went to the chaplaincy who had met her. They all told the same story, Lawrence was a friend of Marvin Brinkmeyer and was a postgraduate student at the university. They all gave the same description, which fits the one you gave and the one in your London nun's letter. The little we know about her was what she told people, and it all leads nowhere. It's all phoney.' Liu could see that the news had gone down badly, so now was the time for the question he'd brought Jimmy here to ask. 'What's your real interest in this?'

Jimmy wasn't ready for it. Liu had intended he wouldn't be.

'What do you mean, real interest?'

'I don't buy you coming here to look into a suicide just because some old friend asks you to. Nobody goes to all that trouble to do someone a favour. My guess is you knew how Brinkmeyer died before you came and from the way it was done you'd be sure it was suicide, so why come? But you do come and while you're here Sr Gray, the one you're supposed to be helping, gets herself murdered. Then your nun friend in London is killed. You turn up here in Vancouver to ask questions and suddenly bad things happen to the people you're involved with. And you're still here, pushing harder and harder. What is it you're pushing for, Mr Costello?'

'I told you, I think Laura Lawrence killed Philomena and

I intend -'

'To pin your nun's death on a woman who it turns out is a phantom. See what I mean? It all happens round you. People die and people disappear.'

Jimmy gave up, his story of why he was in Vancouver was dead and buried. Liu didn't just have all the aces in this game now that Laura Lawrence had gone *phut*, he had the whole fucking deck of cards. Jimmy waited to see which way Liu would jump.

'This is all about something else, something you were working on before you came over here because you came here looking. You know what it is you're looking for, Mr Costello, and we don't.'

Liu was wrong, but he was only wrong in the small print, other than that he was dead right.

'So?'

'So that's my deal. You tell me what this is all about and I share any information I get with you.'

'Is that your own idea or did Brownlow suggest it?'

'I told you, he wants a result. If you have information that can help, fine. But he doesn't want you -'

'Near the case. I know, I heard you tell me. So the idea is that Brownlow puts you at arm's length where the suicide is concerned and you put me at arm's length where any information in the Gray case is concerned.'

Liu nodded. 'Right on the button.'

'And I finish up so far away from any investigation you couldn't see me with a telescope, but I'm supposed to give Brownlow what he wants right up front. Somehow it doesn't sound so very even-handed.'

Liu had the good grace to smile.

'My advice is to take what he's put on offer. Either you do it his way or it doesn't get done at all. Take it or leave it.'

'I'll pass, thanks.'

Liu hadn't expected that, at least not so quickly. He'd

expected Jimmy to try and deal himself closer in.

'You sure?'

'Don't worry, if Brownlow is the good officer you say he is, then it's what he would expect me to say. But I can see how he had to try.'

'We could take you down to the station and do it that way.'

'On what charge?'

'Withholding information. Obstruction of the police.'

Now it was Jimmy's turn to smile.

'Forget it. I co-operated fully at the hotel and I came to you straight away when I had some new information. As for this idea that there is some secret thing behind all of this, you're the only one I've heard float that bright idea. You have nothing. Of course you could always fit me up. You do still occasionally fit people up over here? Or would that be thought too bad-mannered for such a friendly town?'

Jimmy waited. He'd gambled that Liu had been given some wiggle-room. The question was, how much?

'What do you suggest?'

'I suggest that if I knew anything, which I deny, and told you, that would be the last I'd see of you. It's what I would have done when I was in the job and it's what any copper worth spit would still do. Get all the info that's on offer then kick the punter into the long grass. However, if what you mean is, can I suggest a way we could go on meeting, seeing as how both of us have taken such a liking to each other? If that was the case, then I might say, find out if Brinkmeyer was going to become a Catholic and was he interested in becoming a priest? The university Catholic chaplain would know.'

Liu pretended to think about it so Jimmy waited.

'Is that it? Just find out if…'

'I would also say talk to the two who were first at the scene of the suicide and question them properly.' Jimmy leaned forward to make sure Liu got the full message. 'You do know how to do a proper police interview on your own, don't you, without your inspector holding your hand?' Liu didn't like it but he also knew there was nothing he could do about it so Jimmy stood up. 'Go and tell your boss I don't need you but I'm prepared to keep on talking to you if either of you turns up anything that might be of interest, and that means of interest to me, not Brownlow.'

'He won't buy it. Not as it stands. He'd need something more from you.'

'Alright, here's a taster and I'll give it to you for free. Go and see a Mr Felton Crosby, he works for the Catholic diocese and has an office by the Cathedral. I've already talked to him. You could go and ask what we talked about. See you.'

Jimmy went out onto the street which was as busy as it had been inside the bar. What the hell were so many people finding to do out on the streets at this time of night? He decided to walk for a while and think, so he headed back towards the bright lights and traffic of the main road.

Crosby would give them the art angle but beyond that he was a dead end for them. The trouble was, all the other leads were dead ends as well, literally. This Lawrence woman was good. She must have the pictures in her sights and had closed down anything that looked like a threat to her getting them. Oh yes, she was good alright, and dangerous, dangerous as they get. But she wasn't perfect. She'd let him live because she thought he didn't represent any kind of risk to what she was up to, that he was out of it. But he wasn't out of it and he still had New York. Lawrence had no reason to suppose news of a missing New York art dealer would get to Vancouver, any more than a hit-and-run victim in London would, that no-one would make the connections so no one should be looking. But the connections had been made and he was looking. If Lawrence's previous form was anything to go by the art dealer was almost certainly dead, but if he'd shared his bed on a permanent basis then his bedfellow might know something. Please God don't let him turn out to be a celibate bugger.

Jimmy smiled to himself at the unintended joke and felt better. For the first time in this whole mess, he began to feel that maybe he was ahead of Laura Lawrence. But feeling better only lasted until he came out into the harsh lights and traffic noise of the main street. He was ahead of her only if he was right and she'd crossed him off the list of people who mattered in her life.

If he was wrong and Lawrence was still watching him, then soon his name could be added to the body count.

Chapter Twenty-Six

Jimmy hadn't expected to be impressed by New York because, like everybody else, he had seen too many images of that great, restless city to think it could surprise or excite him. And he was right, New York in the flesh was not so very different to the New York of films and TV. The buildings were as high as he had expected, the canyon streets as busy with noisy traffic, the sidewalks as crowded, the cabs as yellow.

As for New Yorkers, they struck him as pretty much like big city dwellers everywhere, a bustling mass, hurrying, talking, getting, doing, and as meaningful to a stranger as a blank brick wall. No, he wasn't impressed, surprised or excited. But he liked the place. It had something of its own, like London, Paris or Rome. It had a character, a style, a sense of what it was: different, unique.

Not that he spent any length of time taking in the sights or sampling the life. Before leaving Vancouver he had looked up Thurlow Somerset's gallery on the internet: Somerset and Tollover Fine Art Dealers, West 24th Street, Manhattan, proprietors Thurlow G. Somerset and Franklyn Tollover. He didn't care about the G, it had to be the Thurlow Somerset he was looking for.

Jimmy asked the cab driver to run him the length of West 24th Street. To Jimmy it was a strange mix and he found it hard to believe as the cab travelled along it that this was in the heart of one of the world's busiest cities. Some blocks were dominated by high-rise apartments, but others were made up of large individual houses which stood in their own grounds. There were plenty of shops but nothing mass-market. The whole street was a curious blend, old and new, the brash and the subtle, functional and decorative. It had no real unity except one: all very expensive, and everybody who did business on this street, the salons, bars, restaurants, boutiques and galleries, all catered to money. Somerset and Tollover were top-end and high-class.

Jimmy paid off the cab a distance from Somerset's gallery and walked. He wanted a final close-up view. There were several galleries on this stretch of West 24th Street, and they were all the same in that their frontages were understated in the way that serious money likes to be when it's out there in the open, where the common herd can get close. When Jimmy arrived at Somerset and Tollover he found it didn't encourage people to walk in and browse, it was a shy place not given to public display. The front window by the door wasn't very big, and in it there were just two large oil paintings on stands, one a rural scene with lots of very green trees, a vivid blue sky with masses of billowy clouds, and small figures doing nothing in particular. The other picture was a jockey in silks and a long-peaked cap, looking out at you while holding the reins of a racehorse. Neither picture did anything for Jimmy except, with the help of some dark drapes behind them, block his or anyone else's view of the interior. He went to the door.

To get into Somerset and Tollover you had to press a button, and a young girl with short, very black hair, pale skin and bright red lips looked at you from a desk near the door, where she was currently working hard reading a glossy magazine. If she liked the look of you she pressed a buzzer to let you in. Jimmy pressed the bell and Red Lips tore herself away from the magazine and looked at him. A voice came out near Jimmy's shoulder.

'Yes?'

'I would like to come in.'

150

'Do you have an appointment?'

'No, no appointment. I'm passing through from Vancouver to London. I'm a friend of Thurlow's.'

Red Lips looked doubtful, but Jimmy's English accent carried the day - or maybe it was that he wasn't wearing a balaclava and carrying a gun. She pressed her buzzer and the door clicked. Jimmy pushed it open. He went in and the door silently closed behind him and clicked shut.

Red Lips went back to her magazine, her duty as Guardian of the Door done, she had lost interest. Jimmy looked around. It was as he had expected, pictures on the walls, vases and statues on tables, wall hangings. An art gallery. It went back quite a way, but the lighting was dim so the far end of the gallery wasn't easy to look into. That seemed odd to Jimmy, why the dim light? People came here to look at pictures, didn't they? On the other hand he'd looked into the windows of the other galleries he'd passed and some of the offerings he'd seen would definitely, to his mind, benefit from dim light. With some of the stuff the dimmer the better.

From the back recesses of the shop a woman came towards him. She stopped by the desk, gave him a look then looked down at Red Lips.

'Who is this?'

The way she said it, it wasn't so much a question as an accusation, but Red Lips shrugged her shoulders as if to say, 'don't ask me, he's your problem now'.

'Well?'

Red Lips made the supreme effort.

'Says he's a friend of Mr Somerset.'

And went back to her magazine.

The woman turned to Jimmy and erected a sort of wintry smile. When she spoke there was frost on her voice.

'Can I help you?'

There was to be no 'sir' for Jimmy. Judgement had been

passed.

Not that he cared. He didn't like the look of her either. She was too old for what she was wearing, the skirt was too short and too tight, the cleavage too low and the colour of the dress too loud. She had on too much make-up and wore too much jewellery. Other than that she was OK. Jimmy could see she liked him as well.

'I'm looking for Mr Somerset, Thurlow Somerset. I'm an old friend from Vancouver.'

The frost turned to ice.

'He's not here.'

She obviously couldn't bring herself to believe people like Thurlow G. Somerset had friends like James C. Costello. She moved round him towards the door. If she was going to throw him out things would get awkward, but the way Jimmy felt about her, he didn't mind awkward.

'One moment, Cynthia.' The woman stopped with her hand on the door handle. From some other part of the gallery a slim man in a lemon-coloured shirt, fawn slacks and tan loafers had appeared. He was, for his age, very good-looking. 'Did you say you were a friend of Thurlow's?'

'Yes, from Vancouver.'

'Vancouver? Then you must know his nephew, Lionel?'

'No, sorry, no Lionel, no anybody, just Thurlow.'

Jimmy hadn't hesitated in sweeping aside what the newcomer had obviously thought of as a clever trap, but his answer seemed to be the right one because good-looking turned his attention back to the Wicked Witch of the West who was still, in hope, holding the door handle.

'Thank you, Cynthia, I'll deal with this gentleman.' Cynthia gave Jimmy a look that dissociated her thoughts on him utterly from the word 'gentleman', and left them to it. 'I'm afraid Thurlow is away at the moment on business. Perhaps I can help? I'm Thurlow's partner, Franklyn Tollover.'

They shook hands. Tollover's was soft and smooth. He must have been sixty but unless you looked carefully he could have easily have passed for forty. Maybe he's never had anything much to worry about, thought Jimmy. Oh well, it's time he started.

'Thurlow Somerset isn't away on business, Mr Tollover, he is missing and has been for some weeks.'

Tollover aged a lot of years in about half a second. This is the bloke, thought Jimmy, this is lover boy. You didn't need to be a trained detective to see that. The pain in his eyes had nothing to do with business. When the pain passed it was replaced by worry.

'Come this way, Mr...?'

'Costello, James Costello.'

Tollover led Jimmy sufficiently far enough away from Red Lips so they could talk unheard then stopped.

'Do you know where he is? Are you a detective, is he...? Is he...' He couldn't get the word out. He was too frightened to even say it.

'Is there somewhere private we can talk?'

'Yes, there's the office.' He turned and Jimmy followed into the back part of the gallery. Cynthia was by a picture which was bathed in lighting from somewhere in the ceiling.

So that's how they do it, thought Jimmy; maybe the stuff is worth looking at after all..

As they approached her, Cynthia began to make a deeper study of a painting. Tollover stopped so Jimmy stopped and looked at the painting. To his unpractised eye it looked like something off the top of a box of chocolates.

'See we're not disturbed, Cynthia.'

Cynthia's back went rigid. She gave up on the chocolate box lid, turned and gave Tollover a look that was a nice blend of anger and betrayal. But Tollover didn't notice and moved on. Jimmy gave her his best smile, the one that never worked like it should.

153

'Yeah, see to it, Cynthia.'

Her look, now directed solely at Jimmy, was a nice blend of loathing and hate. She had a real talent in combining looks but Jimmy didn't wait to appreciate this one. He walked away, following Franklyn Tollover.

Chapter Twenty-Seven

The room at the back of the gallery was part office, part sitting room, and done out like Tollover: good to look at and, even to Jimmy's inexpert eye, all class. A place where the super-rich would be at home while they were parted from their money. Tollover went to a table and poured himself a drink from a bottle of red wine. When he spoke he was back to normal, in control.

'Anything for you, Mr Costello?'

'Do you have any beer?'

'No, sorry. I'm afraid there's no call for beer.'

'Nothing for me then.'

'Please sit down.' They sat down in two leather club chairs beside a dark wood table. 'Do you have any news of Thurlow?'

'He's dead.'

Tollover coughed out some of the wine he'd just drunk, which landed on and soaked into his shirt and slacks. His glass fell from his hand and bounced without breaking on the thick cream carpet, creating a dark stain at his feet and sending dark splashes onto the pale tan of his loafers. His face went into his hands and he sort of crumpled. It had gone down exactly as Jimmy had wanted. Big.

Jimmy waited and after a few seconds the face came out and looked at him. There were no tears and the eyes showed anger rather than pain. Tollover looked at the glass on the carpet by his feet, bent down, picked it up and went to the wine bottle where he poured another. He took a drink, returned to his seat, put the glass on the table and looked at

Jimmy.

Jimmy thought he'd taken it all very well.

Tollover's voice was steady when he spoke.

'You're very direct, Mr Costello.'

'Is there some way you'd have liked it wrapped up?'

'No, I suppose not.' He picked up his glass. 'Are you sure?'

'Yes.'

Tollover took a drink and returned the glass to the table. He was working hard at being in control and not doing so badly.

'May I see the body?'

'There is no body and if it's found you wouldn't want to see it, not after this length of time.'

Tollover looked at the glass, thinking about taking another drink but decided against it.

'Who are you, Mr Costello? You're English so not the police, at least not the NYPD?'

'I'm nobody, nobody official that is. I'm looking into the supposed suicide of a young man who Mr Somerset knew. They both used a chaplaincy to the gay community in Vancouver. I understand Mr Somerset went there a couple of times a year.'

'Then if you're not anybody official how can you be sure that Thurlow is dead.'

'We'll get to that.'

Tollover wiped a hand over the stains on his shirt. He was feeling better. He thought he was back in control.

'I'm not so sure I want to get to that. I think I should call the police.'

'Go ahead.'

Jimmy sat back and waited while Tollover thought about it. Then Tollover also sat back. Now, thought Jimmy, now he's back among the living. Now he's as in control as he's ever likely to be.

'Take a drink, Mr Tollover, you need it and it will help.' Tollover hesitated, but only for a second, then he picked up the glass and finished what was in it. 'Get yourself another.'

Tollover stood up.

'Are you sure you wouldn't…'

'No, Mr Tollover, I'm sure I wouldn't. You have another but then call it quits for a while. Getting smashed will do neither of us any good.'

Tollover went and got his drink then came and sat down.

'I've been to the police, several times in fact. They have no idea where Thurlow is or what's happened to him. There's been no demand for money, no contact of any kind. The police don't seem to be trying too hard to find him.' He leaned towards Jimmy and tried to get as much emotion into his voice as he could. 'I would appreciate any information about him, any information at all.'

Jimmy liked it. Tollover was either a very good actor or he really cared about Thurlow Somerset. But for the moment there were more important things to deal with.

'Why did he go to Vancouver?'

'You're sure he's dead?'

'Yes, and so will you be when I'm finished. Why Vancouver?'

Tollover's manner changed. He seemed to switch off the emotion. It was as if he'd suddenly accepted what Jimmy had told him and found he could live with the news after all.

'I'm afraid Thurlow was in love.'

'There was another man?'

'No, not another man. He was in love with art, it was his only real passion. In particular he loved sacred art from the Renaissance. Many people found that strange because he was a lifelong atheist and for most of his life mocked the faith that had sponsored the art he loved. That the Catholic religion judged him and all other gay people to be no more than perverted hell-fodder may, of course, have had

157

something to do with his attitude. As the Church reviled homosexuality, so he used to revile the hypocritical, pious cant of the Church. But over the years that changed. Slowly he arrived at a conviction that truly great art cannot be based in any way on something totally false. He came to believe that behind the artists who created such masterpieces there was some sort of primal truth which transcended, but could be expressed by, the subject matter they dealt with. He never wavered in his total rejection of conventional piety or the flummery of their rites. But he began to believe that the music and the art Catholic artists had given to the world must have been created by men who were inspired by a knowledge hidden from the rest of us. Some great, mystical truth. Have you ever heard of Gnosis, Mr Costello?' Jimmy shook his head. 'For thousands of years there has been a belief in some sort of secret knowledge, a knowledge hidden from most people. Anyone who could possess that knowledge would have the key to -'

'Can we stick to Vancouver and what he found there or what Marvin Brinkmeyer told him he had found. The pictures. I don't want or need to know about anything else.'

Tollover took another drink. Jimmy could see the transformation taking place. He'd seen it before in so many interviews, when the person being interviewed begins to work out whether or not they have a bargaining position.

'Thurlow wanted to find out what lay behind great sacred paintings. His position regarding religion in general and the Catholic Church in particular was well known in the circles in which we moved. There was no point in trying to talk to anyone in New York about the Catholic Church, and in any case to do so would have seriously prejudiced his position. In our business we live and die by reputation and you cannot do such an about-turn as he proposed and keep your reputation wholly intact. If he wanted to know about the Catholic Church he had to look elsewhere and he came up

158

with Vancouver. He went there and found it give him access to people who could help him in his search. We put the story round that he had a nephew out there, that the nephew was gay and that his family blamed Thurlow and had cut off all contact. As far as the art world of New York was concerned the reason Thurlow went to Vancouver was to see his nephew without his family knowing. About a year ago, on one of his visits, he met Marvin Brinkmeyer and found they shared a love of sacred art. They became friends.'

'Are you sure it was just friends?'

'You're not gay, are you?'

'No.'

'So do you jump into bed with any woman who shares an interest, who might be a friend?'

The last time Jimmy had met a woman who was interested in him that was exactly what had happened. But he could see that now wasn't the time to say so.

'No.'

'Exactly. The last time he came back from Vancouver he was very excited, he told me he had found something stupendous.'

'Some very valuable paintings?'

'It must have been, but he wouldn't say which paintings. He said he wanted it to be a surprise. A special surprise for me.'

'He was going to get these pictures for you?'

'Not exactly. He was going to get the owner of the pictures to let me put them in this gallery and manage the sale.'

'Why was that such a big deal?'

'It was a big deal because he said I would be the one who brought something astounding to the art world.'

'Some lost masterpieces?'

'No, he was the one in love with what you call masterpieces. I deal in contemporary art, what you might

159

call modern art. Our artistic inclinations were very different and complemented each other perfectly - he loved the beauty of the old, I loved the shock of the new. Our success was built on our different -'

'Were these pictures he had found religious pictures?'

'I doubt it. Very little modern art, good modern paintings, are religious works. There are a few of course but -'

'I have reason to believe the pictures are religious pictures.'

'And that reason would be?'

'I can't tell you at this time.'

'For can't, shall I read won't?'

'If you like.'

Tollover didn't like the answer.

'I see. In that case can we get to how you're so sure Thurlow is dead?'

Jimmy ignored the question. He had got the measure of Tollover now. One good punch in the middle of his fancy silk shirt and he would fold. He was soft on the inside as well as the outside.

'What else did he tell you?'

Tollover picked up his glass but didn't take a drink. Instead he held it up and looked coyly at Jimmy over the top of it.

'You know, Mr Costello, I don't think I trust you. I am inclined not to tell you any more.'

'So get Cynthia to throw me out, or better still call the police. I don't give a shit one way or the other because before you do anything else you're going to tell me what you know.' Jimmy could see Tollover believed him, and he was right to believe him because Jimmy couldn't act. But in this case he didn't need to because he meant every word he said.

Tollover finished his drink and made to get up. 'You

don't need another yet, Mr Tollover. Sit down.'

Tollover sat back down.

'If I called out, Cynthia would hear me.'

'And if she was stupid enough to come, Cynthia would get a broken jaw to add to your broken ribs. Where would that get us?'

Tollover gave up. He was frightened and Jimmy didn't blame him. He had beaten confessions out of too many people for his voice not to carry conviction.

'There were fourteen pictures, a sequence of themed studies by a major artist of the later twentieth century. He said that whoever brought them to the art world would become the most important dealer in the world of modern art. It would be the equivalent of discovering a previously unknown series of paintings by Rembrandt.'

Jimmy noticed that his voice was losing its edge of fear as he talked about the paintings.

'So they were valuable?'

'Thurlow couldn't think of how much they might make. Millions obviously, but he had no idea of how many millions.'

'Could they have been stolen?'

'Stolen?'

'Yes, stolen. As in, taken without the owner's permission. That kind of stolen.'

'Of course not. What value would there be in obtaining and displaying stolen pictures? If they were as important as Thurlow seemed to think, they would be recognised, confiscated and we would probably go to prison. No, they were in someone's possession who had no idea of their true value. Thurlow wouldn't tell me who. He said he would make an offer for the paintings. For some reason he seemed to think his offer would be accepted. Then he disappeared. That is really all I know, Mr Costello.'

Yes, it probably is, thought Jimmy.

'You've been frank with me, Mr Tollover, so I'll be equally frank with you.'

'Is this where we get to why you're so sure Thurlow is dead?'

'This is it. Marvin Brinkmeyer found the paintings and told Somerset. Brinkmeyer thought they were stolen, wartime loot. He was going to blow the whistle but before he could do that he conveniently blew his brains out by putting a shotgun in his mouth. Sr Gray, who runs the chaplaincy, thought Brinkmeyer was murdered. Through a mutual friend I was asked to look into it. Before I could get anywhere, Gray was strangled and the mutual friend killed by a hit-and-run driver. The only other living person who knew anything about the pictures was Thurlow Somerset and he went missing shortly after Brinkmeyer's death. Being connected with those pictures, however distantly, seems to have fatal consequences, Mr Tollover. If Somerset let it be known that he was interested in them, maybe even made an offer to sell them, then I would guess he's dead like the others, unless you know some good reason why he would disappear and stay disappeared.' Jimmy stood up. There was nothing more for him here. 'Get some more wine, Mr Tollover, get plenty, I reckon you need it. I'll let myself out.'

Jimmy left the office. In the gallery he passed Cynthia. 'Mr Tollover can be disturbed now, Cynthia. I'm finished with him.'

He could feel the look she was giving his back as he left the gallery. When he got back to the hotel he would have to check his jacket to see if she had left a scorch mark.

Chapter Twenty-Eight

Jimmy sat on the plane heading back to Vancouver. The visit to New York had been good and bad. Good because now he had some idea of what the pictures were, undiscovered masterpieces of modern art, but bad because he still didn't know where they were. And what Tollover had told him was confusing. According to Tollover, the pictures Somerset was interested in were late twentieth century. But the ones Brinkmeyer had been interested in were wartime loot, so they all had to be from before 1945 and some of them must have been old stuff. And Somerset reckoned they were something new and exciting that Tollover could spring on the art world and make a big name for himself. But the stuff he'd been sent to find wasn't new to the art world, the whole point was that the pictures were well-known and valuable.

Nothing seemed to fit, so Jimmy gave up that line of thought. What sort of pictures they were didn't matter until he'd tracked them down. At least now he knew he was looking for a themed sequence of fourteen paintings, which were where they could be seen and studied by people like Brinkmeyer and Somerset but not where people who knew about art would normally go. Where would Brinkmeyer and Somerset go to look at art that other collectors and dealers wouldn't go? Come on, Jimmy, he told himself, you're the great detective. How hard can it be? But nothing came so he tried another tack. Why fourteen? Was fourteen important? Fourteen pictures in a private place but not so private that visits from…

Suddenly a light dawned. Fourteen stolen pictures in the possession of a Catholic diocese who didn't know they had them. Fourteen pictures on display in a place where no one would take any special notice of them as art.

The Stations of the Cross.

It had to be. Every Catholic Church had a set of pictures or plaques representing the fourteen stages in the Passion of Christ, from his trial by Pilate to his crucifixion and burial. But they were devotional things, not looked at as pictures. People went from Station to Station, said their prayers and thought about Christ's Passion. They weren't art, they were the Stations of the Cross.

The Diocese of Vancouver had a set of paintings, modern Stations of the Cross, and under those modern Stations was the stolen art. That meant a church... no, not a church. If they were as important as Somerset thought and out where the public could look at them, their value would have been recognised before now and the stolen art under them discovered. They were in a church or chapel people didn't normally have access to. It had to be a place where you could get permission to go if you had a good reason, but one that was, as a rule, closed to the general public.

The steward came past. The plane wasn't busy and Jimmy had an aisle seat.

'Can I have a beer?'

'Certainly. We have...'

'Anything. You choose. Whatever comes to hand.'

The steward went away.

Jimmy knew it would be some canned or bottled stuff but it would give him something to do with his hands while he thought. His conversation with Felton Crosby came back to him. *People steal paintings to sell them and make money, don't they?* And he was right. Why hang on to something that was wartime loot? Why hide it and keep it? Or was the thief looking for a collector, someone who was rich enough to buy stuff like that just to own it even though he could never let anyone know he owned it? No. A collector, even a crooked one, wouldn't let the pictures go to any church. He'd keep the stuff to gloat over. So why hadn't the paintings been turned into cash years ago? Jimmy realised that was the question that had been niggling at him from the very beginning.

But the question took him nowhere, so he let his brain go into autopilot and waited for his beer. When it came it was a cold can which, when he opened it and poured it, gave him more froth than beer in his plastic glass. God, how he hated flying. He took a drink through the froth, cold and almost tasteless. He should have asked for tea.

What sort of place had the Stations of the Cross on display where the public couldn't get at them but an art history student and an art dealer could see them? It had to be a church. What about some sort of private church, or maybe a chapel? If there was a convent or a monastery or something like that there would be a chapel where the public wouldn't go, but they might let an art student look at their pictures. He was pleased with himself. He was looking for a convent or something like that. But if a convent or monastery had the pictures, how was the Lawrence woman going to get her hands on them? It wouldn't be too hard to rob an ordinary church, but a convent? How did you rob a convent? And if you could, why hadn't it already been done? Why hang about and kill four people while you're hanging about? It all came back to that question. Why were the pictures still there?

Jimmy sat back in his seat. He was tired, tired of thinking, tired of trying to work things out, tired of running around for McBride. What was the point of it all? He had money, he could go anywhere, except that there was nowhere he wanted to go. What use was all the money he'd made without Bernie? He'd only ever been on the take so she could have all the things he thought she wanted. And Bernie had died before she even knew the money was there. There were his daughter and grandchildren, but she'd gone to the other side of the world as soon as she had got married, got as far away from him as she could as soon as she could. She didn't want him back in her life. He couldn't blame her. All he could do for her was stay away. Michael had gone off to be a missionary priest straight from university. That was his way of getting me out of his life, Jimmy acknowledged.

Jimmy thought about Bernie. She had stuck with him even though it meant almost losing her kids. He never realised what staying with him must have cost her, not until she died. Now Bernie and Michael were dead and he lived in Rome pissing about doing McBride's dirty work so the Catholic Church didn't get egg on its face. What the hell was he doing pretending that his life had any meaning just because he kept going through the motions? It was just killing time. A half-smile formed on his lips; at least that sort of killing didn't leave any dead bodies. Then the smile disappeared. It might leave one body. Why kill time, why not just kill yourself and have done with the whole fucking mess? And again the question came, what the hell was he doing with his life?

Slowly his mind closed down. He was very tired, more than just tired, weary and worn-out; weary of it all and worn out by it. The noise of the engines faded and after a few minutes Jimmy slept, and the fizzy beer in the plastic glass in front of him slowly warmed and went flat as the plane headed on for Vancouver.

166

Chapter Twenty-Nine

'It's good of you to see me again, Mr Crosby.'

'Not at all. I'm afraid I can't tell you anything more. The police came and asked me all about it, about what we had discussed. I could tell them nothing more than I told you. I've thought about it but really, I don't think that the diocese has any -'

'No, I don't think so either. But I have to check everything, I have to make sure. Are there any convents or monasteries in or near Vancouver?'

'Yes, there are two convents and one priory.'

'Are they enclosed, not open to the public?'

'The convents are enclosed, yes, but the priory church acts as a parish church.'

'Would the diocese insure any pictures in the convents?'

'No, that would be their own affair, not a matter for the diocese.'

Jimmy stood up.

'In that case I can eliminate them. Thank you for all your help. I think I can say this is the last you'll see of me, that everything has come to a satisfactory conclusion.'

Felton Crosby stood up and came round the desk. He looked relieved as he held out his hand. Jimmy shook it.

'You seem to have been put to a lot of trouble on such an unlikely premise.'

'That Marvin Brinkmeyer might not have killed himself?'

'Oh, no, I'm sorry, I didn't mean the suicide. That, of course, was very sad. I meant that the diocese might have stolen art in its possession.'

'Well, best to run these things to ground. You know what the media can be like where the Catholic Church is concerned. They never let the facts get in the way of a good story. Now, if anyone starts anything about the Church here having stolen art, we know exactly where we stand don't we?'

'Yes. I suppose we do.'

'Goodbye, Mr Crosby.'

'Goodbye, Mr Costello, and thank you.'

Jimmy left and Felton Crosby went back to his desk vaguely puzzled as to what exactly he had thanked Jimmy for.

Jimmy headed back to his hotel. One of those convents had the pictures, he was sure of it. All he had to do was find which one and get a look at their Stations of the Cross. If they were modern, then under them would be the real pictures. Somerset and Brinkmeyer had both got it wrong because neither was a Catholic. They'd both assumed that the diocese was in charge of all Catholic Churches and that included the convents. They hadn't realised that the diocese had nothing to do with the paintings. All they'd managed to do was let Lawrence know they'd found the paintings and knew their value and that got them both killed, and by their blundering around they'd got Gray and Philomena killed as well.

Jimmy didn't care about Brinkmeyer, Gray or Somerset. You didn't care about the victims, it served no purpose; they were just victims, evidence, a part of the puzzle you needed to understand. But he cared about Philomena, she wasn't just a victim to him. Lawrence wasn't going to get away with that particular murder. He'd nail the bitch for that one. But it would have to be by establishing some link between the pictures and the Lawrence woman, some link that would tie her to the pictures and the killings, a link strong enough to get her into court, an unbreakable link. The trouble was, she was good, very good. She had a plan that was worth killing four people to protect. She must be sure that it was foolproof, something that looked legitimate or, better still, actually was legitimate.

Jimmy stopped and looked around. He had no idea where he was. He was just wandering. He saw a taxi and waved it down, gave the driver the name of the hotel and settled back as it pulled away.

Unless he got some kind of break the best he might be able to do was to stop her getting her hands on the pictures. But that didn't give him what he wanted, to pin the murders on her and make sure she spent the rest of her life banged up.

His mind hovered over the question: what would he do if he couldn't get her into court to answer for Philomena? He thought about it. Leave it in God's hands, Jimmy, that's what Philomena would have said, and of course she'd have been right.

But he knew he wouldn't leave it to God. God's justice took eternity and he didn't have eternity. Bernie had believed in God and she'd died of cancer. Philomena had believed in God and Lawrence had run her down and left her to die. God hadn't protected and God wouldn't punish. That only left one option. He'd have to do the job himself. Philomena wouldn't approve, he knew, but he hoped at least she'd understand.

Laura Lawrence had some way of getting those pictures and getting away free and clear. But he didn't want her free and clear. He had to assume that time was not on his side, that Lawrence's plan was already at work. He had to get her before she got the paintings. He wanted her to pay and one way or another, court or no court, he was going to see that she did.

Chapter Thirty

The convent was in an old part of the city, a Victorian fortress of a place whose whole aspect said, 'Keep Out. Nuns Only.' Jimmy pressed the button at the side of the dark wooden door in the arched doorway. He couldn't hear anything but somewhere inside, he hoped, a bell was ringing. After a few minutes the door was opened by an old nun in a full black habit who looked at him suspiciously.

'I've come to see the Mother Superior, Sr Teresa.'

He could see he hadn't convinced her. She still looked suspicious.

'Is she expecting you?'

'Yes, I have an appointment. I phoned yesterday.'

She seemed grudgingly to accept the idea that he might not be trying sneak in and make off with the altar linen, that he might indeed be a genuine visitor.

'What name?'

'Costello, James Costello, I phoned yesterday and -'

'Wait here.'

The door closed so Jimmy waited. After a few minutes the door opened again.

'Come in.' But the way she said it gave him the impression that she washed her hands totally of whatever happened once he was allowed inside.

The floor of the small hall was hard and cold, covered with red tiles, the walls were a sort of institutional cream and damp had caused the plaster under the paint to blister and peel low down in one corner. The old nun led the way into a corridor, again institutional cream and again with hard red tiles. The windows were small, arched affairs with stained glass that let in only a limited amount of daylight, so the few bare bulbs hanging from the ceiling were all switched on even though it was ten thirty in the morning and outside the sun was shining. The whole effect was deeply depressing or profoundly religious depending on your point of view. The old nun went to a door opposite one of the windows and stopped.

'Go in there and wait.'

Jimmy did as he was told and as soon as he got inside the door was closed behind him. At least there was no sound of a key turning in the lock. He looked around the room. There was a small, latticed arched window and the walls were the same grim cream but at least there was a faded carpet on the floor. In one wall there was a forlorn, dusty fireplace that hadn't seen a fire in a very long time. Under the window there was a bulbous black antique radiator. Jimmy went across and felt it. It was cold. Three upright, uncomfortable-looking chairs were at a small rectangular wooden table. Why three, wondered Jimmy? Maybe they represented the Trinity. In the middle of the table was a cheap glass vase with a small amount of greyish water in the bottom of it but no flowers. On the wall opposite the window was the inevitable holy picture. This one was the Sacred Heart, a garish picture Jimmy had known ever since his childhood. Above the fireplace was a large framed photograph of a severe-looking nun dressed in black who looked out accusingly from under elaborate headgear. If you hadn't actually sinned yet, her look seemed to say, you soon would. The room had an air of hopelessness about it but, apart from the fireplace, it was clean. He waited and after ten minutes a nun in, Jimmy guessed, her mid-fifties finally came in and closed the door behind her.

'How do you do, Mr Costello. I'm Sister Teresa.' He obviously wasn't going to get an apology for the wait. The

171

nun pulled out one of the chairs and sat down. 'Please sit down.'

Jimmy joined her at the table. She put a desk diary in front of her and took a pen out from somewhere in the recesses of her black habit. 'Now, when will you come and remove the crates?'

'What crates? I came about the pictures. The Stations of the Cross.'

'Yes. The Stations of the Cross, that's right. The men finished crating them yesterday and I was told you would call to arrange removal.'

Bloody hell, the paintings were on the move. Another day or two and he would have missed them.

Jimmy didn't know what to say, but she held her pen poised over the open diary waiting for him to say something.

'I'm sorry, our wires have got crossed somewhere. I'm not here to arrange moving anything. I just want to ask a few questions about your Stations of the Cross and, if possible, have a look at them.'

The nun looked at him for a second as if she had caught him telling a deliberate lie.

'I see. When you phoned yesterday you said you wished to see me about the Stations of the Cross and I assumed, wrongly as it seems, that you were the man who was arranging their transport. Obviously you are not.' She gave him a wintry smile of apology. 'The mistake was mine.' Jimmy was grateful she didn't fall to her knees and beat her breast. She put away her pen and snapped the diary shut. 'What is it you want about the Stations?'

'Do they belong to the convent?'

She didn't answer straight away. It seemed to Jimmy the question didn't need much thinking about, but that didn't stop her thinking.

'What is your interest in them, Mr Costello?'

Now it was Jimmy's turn to think. Keep McBride out of

it and risk getting kicked out, or give this nun her name and see if it would open any doors. He tried a middle course.

'Some little time ago a young art history student at Vancouver University came to look at your Stations. His name was Marvin Brinkmeyer.'

'Yes, I remember him.'

'Later he either sent, or came here with, an art dealer from New York, Thurlow Somerset.'

'Yes, I remember him as well, although I didn't know he was from New York.'

'I'm afraid one is dead and the other has disappeared.' That got a raising of one eyebrow but nothing more. He tried to remember how he would do this if he was still a copper. 'Marvin Brinkmeyer committed suicide and Thurlow Somerset disappeared not long after Brinkmeyer died. I have reason to believe Somerset's disappearance is connected to Brinkmeyer's death.'

She thought about it again.

'Regrettably people commit suicide and people disappear, but my question is still, what is your interest in the Stations of the Cross?'

Jimmy could see this wasn't going to be easy.

'Marvin Brinkmeyer went to the diocese after he had seen your Stations. He went there to tell them they were in possession of stolen paintings.' Another raising of the eyebrow. Things were warming up. 'Thurlow Somerset, also after seeing your Stations, wrote to the diocese and...' How should he put it? It was tricky. 'Asked to be given first option in arranging for the relocation of the paintings. Of course, the diocese told them both that it had no stolen paintings.'

'Why did they go to the diocese? What has the diocese got to do with our Stations?'

'Neither Brinkmeyer and Somerset were Catholics so they both made the mistake of thinking that any paintings in

173

a Catholic institution must belong to the diocese. They were wrong but that doesn't change the fact that both asserted that the Stations were stolen artworks.'

'Nonsense.'

'Of course nonsense, but just the sort of nonsense the media would love to latch onto, especially given that Marvin Brinkmeyer killed himself and Thurlow Somerset disappeared.' Jimmy could see she was weakening. She couldn't ignore the connection, but Jimmy had to be careful. It wasn't a good story, but it might just scrape past if he didn't try to push it too far. He didn't want to get her thinking that maybe her pictures were anything other than what they seemed. He used what came to hand. 'They were both part of the gay community here in Vancouver.' The inflection in his voice made it sound as if being gay pretty much explained why Brinkmeyer killed himself and why Somerset had disappeared. 'I suspect that Brinkmeyer's death and Somerset's disappearance will turn out to have more to do with that than with any ridiculous stolen art story.'

'But what did they hope to gain by approaching the diocese with such a story?'

Yes, thought, Jimmy, that's just the question I hoped you wouldn't ask. If he wasn't careful he'd get out of his depth and the whole thing would descend into farce.

'I think they were lovers, a young art student and an older art dealer. I'm afraid that sort of liaison goes on all the time among gay people. An older man preys on a younger. The Church's position on homosexuality is well known and the gay community's response to it is equally well known. They may have been hoping to strike at the Church in some way through this story of stolen art in the possession of the diocese. The media would run it whether it was true or not if Brinkmeyer and Somerset both backed it up. I think it was entirely malicious. But there must have been a falling-out.

174

Somerset probably grew tired of Brinkmeyer and threw him over. Brinkmeyer killed himself and Somerset decided he needed a holiday well away from any fuss that might arise from the death and the little scheme they had been plotting.'

He waited. He knew very little about the gay community but he hoped the nun knew less. She was an enclosed nun, but even an enclosed nun who spent her life inside one building among other nuns must have some knowledge of the outside world. It all turned on whether she wanted to believe his story.

'It all sounds thoroughly sordid.'

Jimmy quickly followed up his advantage.

'Yes, I'm afraid it is. I have been asked to look into the matter and make sure that if anyone in the media brings the matter up the diocese can say the whole business has been thoroughly looked into by an independent third party from outside the diocese. Any question of stolen art in Church possession can be quickly and thoroughly refuted. I simply needed to see the pictures to satisfy myself they are what they seem, the Stations of the Cross.'

The nun looked at Jimmy. He wasn't her idea of what an art expert should look like.

'Are you qualified to do that? Do you know about art?'

'I'm a cradle Catholic. I know enough to recognise the Stations of the Cross when I see them.'

It helped but it wasn't enough.

'And why you? You're not Canadian, you're English, aren't you?'

'Yes.'

'Are you a detective of some kind? Do you have any identification?'

'No, I have no identification but I am a detective of some kind. Before I retired I was a detective sergeant in the London Metropolitan Police.'

She was almost there but still not absolutely sure about

him.

'But you are no longer a detective in the London Metropolitan Police.'

'No. I live in Rome. When I retired I went to Duns College.' On hearing about the college that trained mature men for the priesthood, the thaw in her manner was visible. It was just what she needed to take his story on board. Jimmy pressed on. 'After one year I decided that, unfortunately, I didn't have the vocation I'd hoped. But I stayed on in Rome. Occasionally I get asked to look into something, something the Church needs to have handled discreetly. I always act unofficially, you must understand that I do not represent the Church in any official way. I simply look into something and make a report which can be acted upon if necessary.'

He had hoped that his outright denial of any official status with the Church would swing it. It did. Con-men don't force their total lack of status on you.

'Report to whom?'

'There is a monsignor in Rome who liaises on behalf of the Vatican with a senior professor at the Collegio Principe. Between them they, as I said, arrange for certain things that might prove damaging to the Church to be looked into and, if necessary, dealt with.'

'Such as stolen art in Canadian convents?'

That was good, that was almost a joke. He smiled and she smiled back. It was now almost a conversation between old cronies.

'I'd rather not give you the name of the monsignor nor that of the professor at the Collegio, but I can if you insist.'

She gave it one last run in her mind. Certain words and phrases in his explanation made all the difference, especially that snippet of Latin, Collegio Principe. The mixture was too rich to resist.

'No, I will not insist.'

176

Jimmy felt himself relax, he was across the line, but only by a hair's breadth. It had been a damn close-run thing.

'Then if I can see the Stations I will leave you in peace and you can dismiss this unfortunate and, as you say, sordid matter from your mind.'

'I'm afraid you cannot see the pictures. They are crated and awaiting removal for cleaning and then valuation.'

'Valuation?'

'For insurance purposes.'

'But if they belong to the convent you could...'

'They are not the property of the convent. They were loaned to the convent about twenty-five years ago by Mrs Anna Sikora. She is very elderly now and not at all well, I believe. Her son has been given power of attorney for her and he wished the Stations taken away to be cleaned and then valued for insurance purposes.'

'Her son?'

'Yes.'

Jimmy didn't like the idea of a son. He was looking for a twenty-something woman, not a fifty- or sixty-year-old man. He needed time to think so he asked the first question that came into his head.

'When were they last valued?'

'Never that I know of.'

'Never?'

'No. When I became Mother Superior five years ago I found that the Stations weren't insured and apparently had never been valued. To the best of my recollection only two or three of them have ever been removed for cleaning and that was many years ago.'

'What did you do?'

'I thought it was an oversight so I got in touch with Mrs Sikora. But she was adamant that they should not be valued or insured. She said that under no circumstances were the Stations to leave the Convent nor be examined in the

177

convent for insurance purposes except with her express written permission. She assured me that as art they were of no value whatsoever. She also said that even if it turned out they had some small value it was irrelevant. They were works of devotion, that was their purpose and that was the only value she or we should care about. That and nothing else. As I said, she was adamant so I accepted her wishes in the matter. But her son now has power of attorney and he, very sensibly in my opinion, wishes them to be properly insured and prior to valuation has decided they should all be thoroughly and professionally cleaned. They have been taken from our chapel, crated, and are now awaiting collection.'

Bells were ringing. Never valued before but being valued now and being taken away to be cleaned prior to valuation. That had to be the way Lawrence was going to get hold of the stolen art. The Stations might come back, but not the paintings under them. Lawrence would have got her stolen art with nobody the wiser and she'd be free and clear.

'In that case my work in this matter is at an end.' Jimmy stood up. 'If you could give me Mrs Sikora's address, just as a matter of record, I think I can safely say no more will come of this whole sad business and I can go back to Rome to make my report.'

Sr Teresa gave Jimmy the address.

'Mrs Sikora is, as I said, very elderly, and her son says not at all well.'

'That's alright. I don't intend to talk to her. I'll get what I need from the son. It's just to let my monsignor and the professor know who actually owns the pictures. You've been very helpful.'

'Not at all, Mr Costello.'

They stood up. Sister Teresa went to the door and Jimmy followed her. In the corridor he decided he'd have a shot at one last question.

'Were they good paintings, do you think, the Stations?'

'They were both shocking and powerful. It wouldn't surprise me that, despite what Mrs Sikora said, they were in fact quite valuable.'

'Shocking and powerful?'

'Yes, very modern and quite unlike traditional representations of Our Lord's Passion and Death. I remember vividly our reaction here when they arrived all those years ago and were first hung in the Chapel. I was a young novice and had been brought up on traditional Catholic devotional art. To me they seemed almost blasphemous after what I was used to. Most of the older nuns were equally shocked but after a while, as we got used to them, as we prayed in front of them, it became obvious that whoever had painted them had done so with an incredible passion and had drawn from a deep and abiding faith to create them. They were cruel yet compelling, just as Christ's Passion was both cruel and compelling. Slowly I, like the others, came to see them for what they were, a shocking and powerful commentary of the most shocking and powerful event the world has ever seen or will see. Where at first the manner of their depiction shocked and repelled and almost defied you to look at them, slowly they drew you in and began to reveal an inner power, the power of Christ's love seen through his suffering.

'Over the years we have all come to cherish them. They remind us each day that even in the face of Divine Love humanity can still be guilty of the most awful cruelty. One cannot look at them without feeling an impulse to prayer. Christ hanging on the cross is depicted almost like some carcass of butchered meat. As I said, shocking and powerful. Wonderful works of deep devotion. My only reservation about them is that the artist, whoever it was, made the pictures of different sizes. The Crucifixion is the largest and the Agony in the Garden is the smallest. It seems he used size in some sort of metaphorical way, perhaps to express a hierarchy of importance which, of course, would be quite inappropriate. However, nothing can be done about that so we must accept them as they are.'

They'd reached the front door.

'I see. Well I hope you get them back soon cleaned, valued and properly insured. Once that's done any story of stolen art would be too ridiculous even for the Church's most bitter critics to take seriously.'

'Thank you.'

Another nun came into the hall.

'There's a call for you, Mother. Some man about collecting the Stations.'

Jimmy went to the door.

'I'll get out of your way. Once again, thank you.'

'Goodbye, Mr Costello.'

Chapter Thirty-One

Jimmy pulled the heavy wooden door of the convent shut behind him and started walking. The pictures were on the move. He hadn't missed them but it had been close. This had to be what Lawrence was waiting for. Either she knew some way to hijack the Stations for long enough to get the stolen paintings out from underneath, or she'd got the son mixed up in it and would get them through him. Hijacking didn't sound right, it was chancy and she didn't strike him as the kind who took too many chances. Get them through the son? Possible.

If Mrs Sikora was in her nineties the son had to be a good age himself, sixties or seventies. Still, old age didn't stop people being greedy. But Jimmy wasn't at all convinced that Lawrence was the sort to split the goods with anybody. Of course sonny boy wouldn't know that and Lawrence could dispose of him once she had her hands on the paintings and didn't need him any more. What was one more body? He thought about Lawrence. How had she got the son involved? Was it just the money, simple greed? Plain old-fashioned sex wasn't much of a starter. Or was it? More and more he was beginning to understand that where sex was concerned his judgement was badly compromised. She was a lesbian and didn't strike him as anything like a femme-fatale who could lure a foolish old man to his doom. But then again she'd looked like that because she'd been playing a part. That was Laura Lawrence at the chaplaincy. Maybe when she wasn't a lesbian, frumpy, postgraduate English student she looked quite a different Laura Lawrence. She'd killed to get her hooks into the paintings, so providing Sikora's son with the kind of sex he wanted, wouldn't be something she'd draw any line at. If he made it possible for her to get what she wanted, then she'd see that he got what he wanted, whatever it was.

Jimmy walked on until he got back into busy traffic and saw a taxi. He gave the driver Mrs. Sikora's address.

'And on the way stop somewhere I can pick up a pad of notepaper and a pen.'

The driver nodded.

As the taxi headed off, Jimmy reflected on the way the nun had talked about the Stations. She hadn't seemed an overly emotional sort of bird yet those Stations had got right in amongst her. They must be good, bloody good. And she had backed up what Thurlow Somerset had told Tollover: modern and important. Apparently the nun had a good eye for art. Tollover said that they would be a big deal if they got brought out into the open, big enough to put his name up in lights among the art world mandarins. But the Stations on display weren't what this was about, no matter how good they were. Once those Stations left the convent the paintings under them wouldn't be coming back. The nuns would get their Stations back, cleaned and valued, but not until what they covered had been removed. And when that happened the stolen art and Lawrence were going to disappear for good. Time wasn't on his side. Lawrence had a timetable and the whole thing was moving to plan. The crated Stations were on the move and it wouldn't be easy to keep track of them unless he brought in the police, which meant telling them about the stolen art. He wasn't ready to do that unless it became absolutely necessary. Lawrence had to go down, but he'd been sent to sort out the stolen art without any fuss, not to drop it into the lap of the local press via some leaky coppers, so he'd follow his Sikora lead and see where it took him. If the son was…

182

The taxi pulled up. Jimmy looked out. It was a shop selling greetings cards. He didn't want that kind of notepaper but it would have to do.

'I'll be right back.'

The driver waited until Jimmy came back then pulled away. Jimmy put the pack of notepaper and the pen on the seat beside him and looked out of the window. They were leaving the centre of the city and heading towards the suburbs. Jimmy's mind went back to the pictures. Something was wrong. Somerset thought the modern stuff important and very valuable. The nun was obviously deeply impressed by them. When you put her description of the paintings alongside Somerset's you didn't come up with the sort of art whose only purpose was to hide some serious stuff. It didn't make sense. If you want to hide a painting you don't cover it with something that would draw people's attention to it. You cover it with something worthless and God knows he'd seen enough Stations and other Catholic religious art to know it wouldn't have been hard to do. It was a niggle and Jimmy had never liked niggles, too often it meant he'd missed something or gone down the wrong line.

The taxi had moved into a quiet tree-lined street where the houses had enough garden space to be almost classed as 'grounds'. The driver was taking it easy looking for the right address. If this was where she lived Mrs Sikora had the money to make sure she could grow old gracefully.

Jimmy picked up the pack of notepaper, opened it and took out a sheet. It had yellow flowers and bluebirds at the top. He picked up the pen and started to think. This needed to be worded properly. Finally he found the words he wanted and started to write.

When he had finished, something a writer had said on a TV chat show came back to him. He had been asked, what sort of writing paid the most? Ransom notes. It had been a clever reply, but unfortunately it wasn't true. Jimmy looked down at his sheet of paper. There were other notes that could be worth a lot more if you knew where to send them.

Chapter Thirty-Two

The door was opened by a smartly dressed, middle-aged woman. She smiled at Jimmy, another friendly face.

'Can I help you?'

'Could you give this note to Mrs Sikora?' He handed over his note. 'I'll wait here for the reply if there is one.' She didn't seem to want to take the note. 'It's about some pictures, Stations of the Cross that belong to Mrs Sikora. They're on extended loan at the Convent of the Sisters of Perpetual Prayer. I've just come from Sr Teresa, the Mother Superior. She asked me to call but, as Mrs Sikora doesn't know me, I thought I'd send her a note to explain what it's about. Please read it yourself if you wish.'

The maid or housekeeper or whatever she was took the note and opened it. She looked at the note then back at Jimmy. The notepaper didn't match how Jimmy looked, she didn't have him down as the yellow flowers and bluebirds type.

'Sorry about the notepaper. I bought it on my way over.'

She smiled again, Jimmy thought it looked a bit forced this time, but she went back to the note.

Dear Mrs Sikora,

I've been asked to talk to you about the valuation and care of your pictures, both sets, the Stations of the Cross and the other works under them.

James Costello.

The woman seemed reassured but not so reassured that she asked him in.

'Please wait here.' There was no smile this time as she

closed the door. Jimmy waited. A few minutes later the door opened and this time he was invited in.

It wasn't such a very big house, a family of six with servants, a governess and a lot of entertaining to do might have found it a squeeze. Jimmy looked around the hall and at the staircase. Mrs Sikora may have her problems but money wasn't one of them. They went up to the first floor and along a corridor to a door. The woman knocked and went in. Jimmy followed.

He expected to see her in bed but she was neatly dressed and sitting in a comfortable-looking chair by the big bay window. She was small and fragile-looking in that way very old people have. Her hair was white and pulled up. Her hands were folded in her lap. She was old alright, but Jimmy could see no sign of ill-health. In fact, if her eyes were anything to go by, she was good for another ten years at least.

'I understand you want to see me about some pictures?'

Her voice was as frail and fragile as she was, but steady and in control. Jimmy's note hadn't frightened her, whatever else it had done.

'Yes, the Stations of the Cross and the other ones.'

'The other ones?'

'The ones you have been storing. I think it's time they were re-valued. From what I've been told they haven't been valued for a very long time and it's a pity to keep such great art in storage. If they were properly insured they could be brought out of hiding, so to speak, and perhaps put on display somewhere.'

The expression on her bird-like face didn't change and the eyes looking at him were bright. Her body might be frail but she didn't look like a woman who had lost any of her ability to think.

'Well, if we must talk about my pictures I suppose we must. Bring a chair across for Mr Costello, Mary, then you can leave us.'

Mary brought a chair to the window and placed it facing Mrs Sikora. After a little fussing over the old lady she stood up.

'Don't talk for too long, it will make you tired.'

'No, we won't talk too long, will we, Mr Costello?'

'I don't think so.'

Mary left and closed the door behind her. Jimmy sat down.

'What is it you wish to discuss about my paintings?'

'Are we talking about the modern ones, the Stations of the Cross, or the ones hidden underneath them?'

She took the point.

'Please tell me why you have come?'

'A friend of mine in London was killed, someone ran her down in a car. I intend to see that the person who was responsible for her death pays for the crime.'

'And where do my paintings fit in?'

'Your paintings were the reason my friend was killed. A young student at Vancouver University was also killed because of them and a New York art dealer. And there was a nun, Sr Gray, she ran a chaplaincy here in Vancouver.'

The little old lady suddenly seemed to be very much her age and as her head bowed slightly Jimmy noticed that the eyes had lost their brightness. He was worried, maybe he'd misjudged how he told her. Now she didn't look like a sure thing for another ten minutes, let alone years. But slowly she resurfaced.

'That seems a lot of people to die because of some paintings.'

'It is. How much would you say they were worth, the hidden ones?'

'I really have no idea of what they would fetch today, but it would be very many millions of dollars if they were sold on the open market, and probably still millions if they were sold privately to anyone who wouldn't enquire too closely about their provenance. I suppose there are people who would kill several times over for such a sum of money.'

'There are, plenty, and one is here in Vancouver.'

'Do you know who it is?'

'She calls herself Laura Lawrence but that's not her name. She's in her late twenties, short black hair, glasses, medium height, plain-looking. Know her?'

'No, I've never seen anyone who fits that description, but I don't go out these days so unless she came here I wouldn't have met her.'

'How come the paintings are being moved? Why is it important to clean and -'

'Moved?' It was obviously news to the old lady, and unsettling news.

'Yes, they're crated at the convent ready to be taken away. The Mother Superior was told it was for cleaning and valuation.'

'On whose authority?'

'I was told your son's.'

'My son?'

'That's what she said. She said he had your power of attorney and wanted the pictures valued for insurance purposes.'

Mrs Sikora sat thinking about it. She seemed nervous, agitated. Now even a little fearful.

'My son does *not* have power of attorney, and I know nothing about moving the pictures. If I had been consulted I would not have allowed it. I will phone the Mother Superior and stop it.'

'Can you?'

'They are still, legally, my paintings.'

'Yes, but the Mother Superior says your son has power of attorney. I assume she has seen the necessary paperwork and if he says they go I don't see how the Mother Superior can stop it. Could your son have got power of attorney without your knowledge?'

She thought about that for a second.

'He brings me papers to sign. I used to read them all carefully but over the last few years...' She made a small dismissive gesture with one hand. 'One gets old, tired, becomes careless or too trusting.'

'That's a yes then, is it?'

She gave a single nod.

'I suppose it's possible that I signed something without realising what it was.' They sat for a moment. Jimmy let it sink in, that her son was trying to cheat her, to steal from her. She needed time to adjust. He had to be careful. He didn't want her too tired or too upset to give him what he wanted. When she spoke Jimmy got the impression that she was trying to work something out. 'You say this woman Lawrence killed all those people, that she is after the money. How does she expect to get hold of the pictures?'

'I don't know, but she's very sure she will. Somehow your son and this Lawrence woman have got together to get hold of the stolen art. I have no idea how she might have involved your son but she has. If the arrangements for the Stations to leave the convent go ahead than my guess is you won't see the paintings under them again. They'll be removed. The Stations will be re-framed then cleaned and valued. Apart from you, how would anyone know that anything had been taken?'

The old lady seemed to pull herself together, her head came back up and her eyes were bright again.

'Then the Stations mustn't leave the convent. All that must be stopped.'

Good for you, thought, Jimmy.

'Fine, but don't tell me, I can't do anything, tell your son. Confront him with what you know about the power of attorney and remind him that he's already committed a

189

criminal offence. And then ask him to explain where Laura Lawrence fits in. When he knows he's blown I'm sure he'll see the wisdom of co-operating. If he tries to be difficult tell him he stands a good chance of being charged with being an accessory in four murders. If he didn't know about them before, and he probably didn't, make sure he knows about them now.'

'I would rather it didn't go that far. If it is at all possible I would want the police kept out of it.'

Yes, thought Jimmy, I can see how you'd want that. Your son has committed fraud, got himself mixed up with a multiple murderer and is about to get hold of some stolen art that you have been sitting on for God knows how long. I wouldn't want the police involved either if I were you. Not that it mattered. Keeping the police out of it until he was ready to drop Laura Lawrence into the lap of Brownlow and Liu for murder was exactly the way he wanted it. When he was ready for that they could have the whole thing, Mrs Sikora, the son, the stolen pictures, the whole lot. Time had run out on trying to keep McBride and the Catholic Church happy.

'Maybe the police needn't be involved if he spills everything he knows about Laura Lawrence. All I need is Lawrence for the London murder. I don't care about the rest, the other killings or the pictures. Can you contact him?'

'Yes.'

Jimmy took out his mobile and held it out.

'Go ahead.'

'I'd rather talk to my son in person, and when I do I want to talk to him alone.'

Jimmy put his mobile away.

'That's OK by me so long as while you're talking to him you make sure to find out how he's mixed up with the Lawrence woman and where they were going to take the Stations so they could get the pictures they wanted.'

'What makes you so sure he is involved with this woman? Couldn't she just be using him?'

'He fiddled the power of attorney, he committed a crime. He's involved alright, he has to be. Using him is her only way to get at the pictures and get out free and clear. If he's moving the pictures it's because she's arranged it with him.'

'Yes, I suppose he must be involved with her.'

'And I wouldn't hang about, she's killed four times and I don't get the impression she's the type who would be prepared to go halves once she's got her hands on what she wants - or leave anybody around who could point the finger at her.'

'You think she may kill again?'

'Yes, I think she will.'

She sat looking at her hands in her lap. She was thinking. Jimmy could see that something wasn't right. He'd told her all she needed to know yet she was still thinking. Eventually she surfaced.

'And you, Mr. Costello, what will you do if I get you the information you want?'

'I just want the Lawrence woman in court for murder.' He waited but she was still thinking. 'I'll keep your son out of if I can. I'll do my best but I can make no promises.'

He told the lie well, it wasn't acting, it was practice, something left over from his CID days, a throwback to the many times he had interviewed people and told them that same lie, 'tell me what I want and I'll keep you out of it'. So they told him and he dropped them straight in it.

'I'll talk to my son and then call you.'

She'd come to some sort of decision and wanted him gone.

'Mrs Sikora, I've been open with you. I've told you what I know and I haven't involved the police.' There was no way she could know that he had. 'If you know anything or even if you only suspect something I would advise you to share it

191

with me.'

'What could I know? As you see I am unable to leave the house, I am barely able to leave this room, and when I do so it is only with the help of Mary or my son. Your news about my son and the power of attorney came as a complete surprise to me, as did this business of the woman you suspect murdered all those people. What could I possibly know?'

Jimmy stood up. If she was digging her heels in there was no point in pushing. Any pressure and she might conk out on him, and he needed her to get in touch with the son as soon as she could. The son was the one who'd get the pressure applied if he didn't want to co-operate. Anyway, the most important thing now was to put a stopper on the paintings moving. They would have to be moved at some point for Lawrence to show, but Jimmy wanted time to be ready when it happened. When Lawrence surfaced again he wanted to be there.

'You can get me at the Rosedale on Robson.'

'I will call you this evening. Please see yourself out.'

'I'll wait for your call, and remember you need to get this done quickly.'

'I will, Mr Costello. I will deal with it as soon as you have left.'

Jimmy turned and walked to the door. He looked back. The bright little eyes were watching him and he was sure her bright little brain was ticking, but whatever was going on in her head he had to leave it as it stood. He closed the door gently behind him.

Back down in the hallway Mary came out of a room as he got to the bottom of the staircase.

'Do you have the number of a taxi firm? It's too far to walk back to my hotel?'

'Certainly.'

Mary left and came back a moment later with a small

notebook. She read out a number and Jimmy tapped it into his phone. The cab company answered. He gave them the address and put away the phone.

'She seems very well for her age, I hope I didn't stay too long.'

'She is very well for her age and, no, you didn't stay too long. She enjoys short visits but she doesn't get many.'

'Just her son, I suppose?'

'No, he doesn't visit.'

'No?'

She smiled.

'He doesn't need to, he lives here.'

She'd caught him out, it was her idea of a little joke. Jimmy forced out a smile.

'I see. Well, goodbye. I'll wait outside for the taxi.'

'You're more than welcome to sit in the living room.'

'Thanks, but I think I'd like to wander up and down in the sunshine until my taxi arrives. It's a nice neighbourhood.'

Mary went and opened the door.

'Goodbye, Mr Costello.'

He went out and the door closed behind him. He walked down the path, through the gate and onto the street. It was a quiet place with almost no traffic, he could stroll about and think until the taxi came. He'd picked up another niggle. He'd missed something up there in the old lady's room, or got something wrong. But what? All he could do was go back to the hotel and wait for her call. It was slow, hard work but he was sure he was close. A day or two and he'd get his chance. It wasn't the way Philomena would have wanted, but it was what he wanted, and right now it was what he wanted that counted.

Chapter Thirty-Three

The call came at seven p.m.

'Mr. Costello, could you come and see me?'

'When?'

'Now.'

'Now?'

'Yes, now.'

'Sure. I'll be with you in about twenty minutes.'

'Thank you.'

From the tone of her voice she'd had her talk and it hadn't gone well. Still, if you're confronting your son with attempted theft and being an accessory to multiple murders, you don't expect sweetness and light, do you? How could it have gone other than badly?

Jimmy went down to the street and found a taxi. The evening traffic was beginning to pick up and the bright lights of the night were coming on although as yet it wasn't dark. In the suburbs the last cars of those who worked late were making their way home to the expensive, comfortable houses which soaked up the money from all those late hours. Jimmy paid off the taxi, went to the front door and rang the bell. Mary opened it and stood to one side for him to enter. There were no words of welcome and no smiles this time, she just closed the door behind him and led him upstairs. At Mrs Sikora's door she knocked then turned and walked away. No, thought Jimmy, it didn't look as if things had gone at all well.

Mrs Sikora was sitting in the same chair but now the curtains were closed and a table lamp was on. She looked pretty much the same except her eyes weren't so bright. There was a chair waiting opposite her so Jimmy closed the door and went and sat down.

'Please tell me what your interest in all this is, Mr Costello.'

'I told you, a friend of mine...'

Her bird-like head shook impatiently.

'Mr. Costello, please don't waste my time, God knows I have little enough of it left. Forget your friend for a moment and tell me what it is you're doing here in Vancouver.'

Jimmy decided that there was no point in pissing her about.

'I was sent to look into a claim that the Vancouver Roman Catholic Diocese was in the possession of stolen art. You and I know that's not true because the art in question belongs to you, not the Church. The people I told you about earlier, the student, Marvin Brinkmeyer, and the art dealer, Thurlow Somerset, were allowed to study the paintings that covered the stolen pictures and found out what was under them. That got them killed. Sr Gray knew Marvin Brinkmeyer, she was trying to persuade the police his death wasn't suicide -'

'I thought you said he'd been murdered.'

'I think he was, but the way he was killed...'

Jimmy paused. It wasn't a pretty thing to describe to a frail old lady.

'Yes, yes, the way he was killed. Go on.'

'He put a shotgun in his mouth and blew a good part of his head off.'

Jimmy waited, but the old girl didn't even blink.

'It certainly sounds like suicide.'

'That's what I thought originally and what the police still think. But now I'm fairly sure Laura Lawrence killed him somehow.'

'I see. And your friend in London?'

'She knew Sr Gray. They'd been on a conference together and Sr Gray had told her all about Marvin Brinkmeyer. She was the one who got me to come here and start asking questions.'

'But you said you had been sent to look into the paintings, not into some suicide.'

There was nothing wrong with the old girl's faculties. She had a mind that could stay bang on track.

'I was, but I needed a reason to be here and nose about. Looking into the suicide for a friend of a friend… Anyway, it held the police for a while, and when Sr Gray was killed…'

'The police have questioned you?'

'Yes, but as I said, my story was good enough so they weren't a problem.' The lies were piling up and he didn't like it. Keep on lying to a sharp old bird like this and pretty soon he'd trip himself up. He had to take charge. 'Mrs Sikora, I've tried to keep the art out of this so far and that means I've kept you and your son out of it, but now I need you to tell me what your son said about the pictures and Laura Lawrence.'

'He denies any knowledge of this Laura Lawrence.'

'I see. You told him you knew about the phoney power of attorney?'

'Yes, but he says he told me what the papers were for when he brought them to me for signing.'

'But you don't remember that he did.'

Mrs Sikora gave a slight shrug.

'Your memory seems fine to me.'

'When you're my age you must expect the odd lapse. He might have told me. It's possible.'

She was covering for him, Jimmy was sure of it. But how to get round it?

'Did you tell him to stop moving the pictures?'

'No.'

'No?'

'He explained that. He said he knew I didn't want them moved so he didn't tell me. But he feels that they really ought to be cleaned. Something about candle smoke in the convent chapel. And while they were out of the convent he thought it best to have them valued for insurance purposes. He felt I was being unfair to the Sisters in not having them insured. If anything happened to the Stations and it turned out they were indeed valuable the Sisters might he blamed. He said he didn't want me worried about it so he didn't tell me.'

'Do you believe him?'

There was a pause. She was making up her mind which way she would go. All Jimmy could do was wait.

'No. I think he was lying. I think he intends to remove the stolen paintings while the Stations are out of the convent, then he will get the Stations cleaned, valued and returned with no one the wiser.'

Jimmy could see the pain it was causing her to say it to a stranger, that her son was stealing from her. Still, now she'd decided which way she was going he had to get the whole story out of her, the true story.

'Did you give him power of attorney?'

'It was something we had talked about quite a lot. I am nearly ninety years old, how much time do I have left? If I died suddenly I wanted to be sure the pictures would be,' she looked for the right words, 'that they would continue to be taken care of as I would wish. I told my son I was considering power of attorney about twelve months ago. I asked my lawyer to draw up the papers.'

'So he knew about them?'

'Oh yes, in case they were needed.'

'What are you going to do about it?'

'What can I do? He has power of attorney. Even if I could get to the convent, what difference would it make?'

'You could revoke the papers.'

'Assuming I could, which is a big assumption, the pictures would almost certainly be gone before it came into effect.' She was right. The son and the Lawrence woman were going to get their bloody stolen art unless he could think of something and think of it damn soon. Now in fact. 'What do you suggest I do, Mr Costello?'

'I could stop him.'

'Would that involve violence?'

'Yes. If I put him in hospital that should stop things.'

He could see she didn't like the idea but he hadn't really expected her to. What mother would?

'I must think about it, Mr Costello. I will try to see that the pictures do not leave the convent in the next couple of days. I will contact the Mother Superior tomorrow but the best I can hope for is a short delay. I will talk to my lawyer and do what I can. You understand I want no harm to come to my son. I do not want any…'

She didn't know how to say it.

'You want him out of it with the least amount of grief to you or him.'

'Yes.'

'OK, try and stall the pictures and I'll have a word with him. If he tells me where the Lawrence woman is I'll deal with her.'

'I would rather there was no violence.'

'OK, I won't tell you about it.'

She looked at him with eyes that were now filled with sadness.

'Do you have children, Mr Costello?'

'Does it matter?'

'No, I suppose not. Each family is unhappy in its own way. Finish it then, finish it in any way you can.'

'And your son?'

'He is my responsibility.' She reached across to a drawer

in the table by her chair and pulled it open. From it she took a bulky brown envelope wrapped round with strips of sticky tape. She lifted it with both hands onto the table. That was as far as her frail strength could get it. She pushed the drawer shut. 'Take it, Mr Costello.'

'What is it?'

She looked at the envelope then back at Jimmy. There were tears in her eyes.

'It's my life story. If anything happens to me I would like you to read it.'

'And do what?'

'Whatever you think proper.'

'I don't want it. Your life is nothing to do with me one way or another. All I want is the Lawrence woman.'

The first tear left her eye and ran down her cheek but she smiled. A gentle smile, a real smile.

'It is my price, Mr Costello. Take it and read it or I will let the pictures go.'

Jimmy didn't hesitate for long. He reached out and took the envelope. But he didn't say he'd read it, that was her idea not his.

'When will you call the convent?'

'Tomorrow morning. Then I will call my lawyer.'

'And when do I get to have my chat with your son about the woman?'

'I will phone you before ten tomorrow.'

'I'll be waiting for the call.'

She said nothing, just lowered her head so that she was looking down at her hands folded in her lap. She seemed to have shrunk since they had met earlier in the day. She was tired - no, not tired, withering away, drying out before his eyes, finished. The Lawrence woman would be able to add one more to the body count before long.

Jimmy stood up. She didn't look at him so he left, closing the door quietly behind him. He went downstairs and out of the front door. He met no one on the way out. The house seemed empty, deserted, as if someone had recently passed away there. Maybe in a way somebody had.

Chapter Thirty-Four

Jimmy stood at the window of his suite and looked out on the now-familiar scene. There was rain sweeping across the bay and North Vancouver was hidden from view. He looked at his watch again. It was half-past ten and no call had come. Had she changed her mind? Had the son changed it for her? Or was she just late getting in touch? If she was up to something, he needed to know what it was. He went down to the Reception desk and asked for a local directory. He took it to the bar and laid it out on a table. There she was, Mrs. A Sikora, at the right address. Jimmy sat back and took out his phone. It was Mary who answered.

'Hello, this is Mr Costello, I called yesterday, twice. I came to talk to Mrs Sikora about some paintings. I was expecting her to get in touch this morning but…'

'I'm afraid Mrs Sikora passed away peacefully in her sleep during the night.'

Jimmy could hear the tears in her voice.

'I see, I'm very sorry. Please pass on my condolences to her son.'

'I will.'

'Was he with her when she died?'

'No, I told you. She died in her sleep. I found her when I went to her room at about seven thirty this morning.'

If the shock of the sudden death had made her willing to talk, Jimmy decided now was a good time to get what he could.

'Did Mrs Sikora have any other visitors after I left?'

'No, no one.'

'Could anyone have got in without your knowing?'

There was a pause. Her brain was clicking back in.

'No. Why do you ask?'

'You say she died in her sleep. Was there any sign of a struggle?'

No answer.

'Have the police been informed?'

That brought her back.

'The police?'

'A sudden, unexpected death? Surely the police are usually informed?'

'Young Mr Sikora is seeing to everything. I'm sure he will do whatever is necessary.'

The interview was over. She was back in the land of the living and Jimmy knew he'd get no more information.

'Thank you and once again, my condolences.'

The phone went down without any reply.

So, the old lady had conveniently died. Now there was no way of stopping the pictures moving. Jimmy thought about the son. Would he go ahead now that his mother was dead? Mary's words came back to him: 'Young Mr Sikora'. Funny how domestics give people these titles and they stick. How old would sonny boy have to get before he stopped being 'Young Mr Sikora'? Jimmy went back to the death. It couldn't be a coincidence. The old lady died at just the right time, after she found out what was happening but before she could do anything. It had to be murder. But how the hell had the Lawrence woman got at her? Unless it was the son, but that didn't sound likely. An elderly, single man still living with his mother, he might steal her paintings if he got put up to it, but kill his own mother? Jimmy changed the direction of his thoughts.

Forget the old lady, forget the son and even forget Laura Lawrence for the moment. What mattered was those bloody pictures. If they left the convent then he was well and truly fucked. Mrs Sikora's words came back to him: "Then they mustn't leave the convent". Too true, old lady, too absolutely, fucking true.

Jimmy picked up his phone again, found the number he wanted and dialled.

'Sr Teresa please, it's Mr Costello.' There was a pause then her voice came on.

'Yes, Mr Costello, what can I do for you?'

'Mrs Sikora is dead. She died last night, passed away peacefully in her sleep. Mary, the housekeeper, found her this morning.'

'I see.'

'Are her pictures, the Stations, still with you?'

'Yes, they are being collected this afternoon at two.'

'I wouldn't go ahead with that.'

'Why not?'

'If Mrs Sikora is dead then the pictures now belong to her next of kin or whoever she left them to in her will.'

'But her son has power of attorney, if he wants…'

'Power of attorney ceases on death. You shouldn't release those pictures from the convent until you know who owns them and you won't know that until Mrs Sikora's will is read or, if there is no will, until probate is completed.' There was a silence while she thought about it. He needed her to hang on to the pictures. 'At the very least I think you would be well advised to take legal guidance. Of course you must do whatever you think is right. I just thought I would mention it. Is there someone from whom you could get suitable advice?'

Another pause.

'Yes, there is someone.'

Her voice was hesitant. She didn't like it. Too much was happening too quickly. Jimmy knew he needed to ring off before she started thinking and asking any questions.

'Good. In that case I'll let you get on with it.'

Another pause, then.

'Thank you, Mr Costello.'

'Not at all, goodbye, Sister.'

And the phone was down before she could reply. Thank God she hadn't asked him how he knew about Mrs Sikora's death. Jimmy put his phone into his pocket then took the directory back to reception. He went back up to his suite, made himself a cup of tea and went to the window. The rain must be easing off, the vague outline of the mountains across the bay was just becoming visible. What to do now? If he had persuaded the Mother Superior to stop the removal of the pictures, that had bought him time. But if the Mother Superior did hold on to them and decided they couldn't be moved until the will was read or probate sorted then he'd got himself too much time. If the pictures got stuck in the convent for weeks, maybe months, he had no way of knowing how or when Laura Lawrence would surface or even if she would surface. And he couldn't very well hang around Vancouver until the business of who the Stations belonged to got sorted.

Shit. He'd got himself out of one hole and dropped himself in another.

He finished his tea and put the cup in the sink. What now? Bring in Brownlow and Liu? What could they do except go and look at the Stations and confirm the stolen art under them, and once Lawrence knew the police were involved she would disappear for good. No, that way was no good to him. Lawrence wouldn't get her paintings but nor would she receive punishment for Philomena. Jimmy wasn't ready to let it go at that.

If not the police that only left the son.

Time to meet 'Young Mr Sikora' and age him a little.

Chapter Thirty-Five

The taxi pulled up at the Sikora house just as a man in his mid-to-late twenties, wearing a dark overcoat, was getting into a black panel van. Jimmy paid off the taxi and it pulled away behind the van.

Jimmy went to the door and rang the bell. Mary answered.

'Mr Costello.'

She didn't look glad to see him.

'Is Mrs Sikora's son at home?'

'Mr Lawrence? No, you've just missed him. He's gone with his mother's body to the funeral parlour to make arrangements.'

Jimmy looked round but the van was out of sight. Mr *Lawrence*? The man in the dark coat? A man in his twenties?

'How old is Mr Sikora?'

'Twenty-eight. Why do you ask?'

Jimmy ignored the question.

'May I come in for a moment?' Mary looked doubtful but she didn't close the door. 'I really do think we need to talk. I was helping Mrs Sikora with a problem that has arisen over a set of Stations of the Cross which she loaned to the Convent of the Sisters of Perpetual Prayer some years ago. Now that Mrs Sikora has sadly passed away I will have to deal with someone else.'

'Mr Lawrence?'

'Yes, Mr Lawrence Sikora. Of course he is very busy now and it would be intolerable to intrude on his present

205

grief, but if I could get some background from you... Nothing personal, you understand, just information I will need to write up my report. Mr Sikora will of course get a copy.'

'Who is it that you represent exactly?'

'I'm quite happy for you to know that, but do you think we might talk inside?'

Mary paused only for a moment then stood to one side.

She took him into the living room off the hall. It was a big, airy room with large bay windows. Everything looked solid, expensive and tasteful. Mr Lawrence obviously stood to inherit a packet, not to mention some valuable modern Stations and some dodgy old masters.

'Who is it you represent, Mr Costello?'

'The Roman Catholic Diocese of Vancouver. I have been retained by Mr Felton Crosby to do an inventory of all art works that may have significant value and as yet have not been insured.'

It was a good lie given the short notice.

'But you said Mrs Sikora had loaned them to the convent? Wouldn't the Sisters…?'

'No, even though they are in the convent chapel, the responsibility for insurance still rests with the diocese. It has only recently come to Mr Crosby's attention that the Stations are not in fact insured. That is why I was brought in and why I came to see Mrs Sikora. I have to make a full report on condition and likely value and make a recommendation to Mr Crosby. Needless to say I didn't want to do that without informing and getting the agreement of the legal owner, Mrs Sikora. Now I must inform and get the agreement of Mr Lawrence…' Jimmy paused for effect. This was the crunch. 'Once I am sure he is the legal heir to Mrs Sikora's property.'

He let Mary digest his story. She'd need a few minutes, after all, it was quite a lot to swallow.

'I see. So you want me to…?'

'To fill in a little preliminary background. Nothing too personal and nothing at all private. Just enough for me to take to Mr Crosby and get permission to carry on with my report and deal with Mr Lawrence now that his mother, sadly…'

Jimmy left it hanging. It was a good line to finish on.

'Well, if I can help.'

Jimmy tried to sound diffident.

'I'm not sure how to put this…' Pause for effect, 'Oh well, I might as well be direct. If Mrs Sikora was nearly ninety, then how is it that she has a son so young?'

'Young Mr Sikora was adopted.'

'I see. Do you have any idea of when Mr Lawrence was adopted?'

'About eighteen years ago I think, but I don't know for sure.'

'And you came to the house when?'

'Nearly ten years ago.'

'You live here?'

'Yes, it was a residential position, cook, housekeeper and after a few years, companion.'

'Companion?'

'I became her companion. There was no money involved, no payment. I was glad to be a friend. Mrs Sikora was, I think, a lonely person.'

'She had her son, her adoptive son? Wasn't he a companion?'

'He lived with her here in the house, but they were not what I would call close. She needed a woman, someone to talk with, to share…' She seemed to be worried that she had said more than she should. 'As far as I am aware she had no other family. There was just myself and young Mr Sikora. I was paid, I was a servant, but I think I was also a friend.'

Jimmy sensed that he had got all he was going to get.

'I'm sure you were indeed a good friend and a good companion.'

'I hope so.'

'You have been very helpful. I think from what you have told me, that I can continue with my work. I will make my report to Mr Crosby and say that from now on Mr Lawrence Sikora will be the one I will deal with here. Can I leave a message for him?'

'Of course.'

'As soon as he comes back can you give him the note I gave you for Mrs Sikora? He will be the one I will have to talk to about the pictures now.'

'Well, I don't think he would want to talk about pictures at this time. I'm sure he will have too much…'

'If you would just find the note and give it to him. Tell him it was the note I gave to his mother and we talked, talked fully about the pictures.'

'That you talked about the pictures?'

'Yes. Tell him his mother and I talked fully about the pictures. I'm sure he will understand.' She was freezing up again but Jimmy didn't mind. He'd got where he wanted to go. She'd given him all he needed. 'Please tell him that, use those words if you can. It will make things clear to him.'

'If that is what you wish.'

Jimmy tried to smile.

'Yes, it is what I wish. If he wishes to see me, when he is ready of course, I am staying at the Rosedale on Robson.'

'But I thought you worked for the Vancouver Diocese?'

'I am a consultant. I live in Toronto.'

'I see.'

'Obviously I don't want to hurry Mr Sikora but my time here is limited. Tell him I understand that things have become very difficult for him but that when he is available I think we should meet.'

'I will.' She went to the door and opened it. 'There is a

lot to do.'

'Of course. So much to do.'

Mary led him out of the living room to the front door.

'Goodbye, Mr Costello.'

It sounded final.

Jimmy walked down the path to the front gate. He wanted to get back to the hotel and get things sorted. There wasn't much to do but he wanted to make sure it was done right. If there was going to be blood on the carpet he wanted to make sure it was the right blood and the right carpet and that everything else was in place to deal with it once it was spilt.

Mr Lawrence, Young Mr Sikora, Laura Lawrence.

It had all been there if he'd done his job properly from the beginning, but he hadn't even got a sniff of it until now. It had been a good plan alright, a bloody good plan. But now it was all out where he could see it, all he had to do was push the right button and it all fell into his lap. The bastard would pay. God hadn't protected and God wouldn't punish. But someone had to punish, and he was that someone.

When he had got back to the hotel, he had told Reception that he wasn't feeling too well, that he wanted to rest. If anyone asked for him could they say he was out but had said he would be back shortly after five? Of course they could.

He needed time to get ready, to put everything in a neat row so that when the first block fell all the others tumbled neatly after it. Back in his suite Jimmy sat nursing a cup of tea. On the table beside the saucer was the empty brown envelope and scattered across the table were the pages it had contained. Each page, on both sides, was covered with small, neat handwriting, Mrs Sikora's life story. He was reading it because now it was the only way she could talk to him and he needed to know what she had to say.

Chapter Thirty-Six

My name since 1945 has been Anna Sikora but I was born Miriam Feldstein. My family lived in Baranowicze in Eastern Poland. We were Jews. Baranowicze had almost thirty thousand inhabitants, Jews, Poles, Belarusians and Russians, and it was the most important and prosperous town in the Nowogródzkie Province. I remember my childhood as a happy one. We lived in a small, terraced house in a poor district not far from the barracks of the Nowogródska Cavalry Brigade. My father was a boot-maker with a small but secure living making boots for the junior officers at the barracks. My mother worked as a cleaner in some of the big houses of the wealthy Jews, of whom there were many. I had two older brothers, Simon and Elias. They helped my father with his boot-making and I helped my mother with her cleaning work.

That was how I became friends with Sarah. We were the same age and when I went with my mother to Sarah's house we would play together. She was an only child and her parents, who were kind people, liked her to have a friend with whom she could play. Sarah was a cripple, she had contracted polio when very young and was confined to a wheelchair. Her family were very rich, her father was a merchant and had many contracts with the military in the town, the Border Protection Brigade, the 20th Infantry Division and the Cavalry Brigade whose officers bought my father's boots. They lived in a big house with many fine things.

Sarah's father was a cultured man and had a great love

of art, which Sarah had inherited. He had a fine collection of paintings and I would spend many hours wheeling Sarah from picture to picture while she explained to me how wonderful each one was. I had no interest in the pictures but I had a great love of Sarah so I pushed and listened and tried to sound interested. I visited Sarah often as we grew older and we became more like sisters than friends. Sarah was educated at home and her father had been keen that although she was too delicate to travel herself, she should be able to travel in her mind through art and literature. He arranged for her to have lessons in Russian and English; Russian to talk to our eastern neighbours and English to talk to the world. I was allowed to join in Sarah's language lessons so that she would have a companion to talk to and so learn more quickly. Sarah didn't like the language lessons, they bored her, but I enjoyed them and between us we made good progress. I would sometimes stay at her house for a whole week and, once, the family took me with them when they went on holiday to the country. That was the happiest time of my life.

The next year the war came. The Red Army arrived and took over everything. The Polish army seemed to melt away from the town. The Jews of Baranowicze welcomed the Soviet troops. We had all heard of what was happening to Jews in Germany and although it was bad to come under the Soviets it would be much worse to be under the Nazis. Children went into the parks to pick the flowers to give to the soldiers as they arrived. The troops settled into the barracks and life more or less went on for a while. Sarah's father came to some sort of agreement with them about supplies and my father and brothers found work repairing the soldiers' boots. The soldiers' boots were of very poor quality and gave my father and brother plenty of work although the pay was poor and didn't always arrive, so things didn't change for us so very much. The Soviets didn't seem to care one way or the other about Jews so we made the best of it and thanked God that it was the Red Army who had come and not the Wehrmacht. There were nearly ten thousand Jews in Baranowicze and not long after the Soviets took over another three thousand Jewish refugees arrived who had fled from Western Poland in front of the German invasion. The stories they told made us thank God even more. Then, in June 1941, the bombing began and the Germans invaded. We found ourselves gathering what we could and became refugees heading east, away from the Germans.

Everything was chaos and on the fifth day on the road I got parted from my family. I looked for them but it was hopeless. The Luftwaffe were bombing and strafing the roads and when the planes weren't attacking us we were driven off the roads to make way for the Red Army, which seemed to be going both ways at once, reinforcements coming to the front and convoys of retreating men and supplies. It was a time of madness. I continued to make my way east, always looking for my family, but I never saw any of them again.

Eventually, after almost two weeks on the road, I arrived at a village where there was a group of three Red Army lorries. There were five men under the command of a corporal, they were sitting by their lorries cooking a meal. I knew that if I carried on walking I would soon die. I spoke Russian so I asked if they would take me with them wherever it was they were going. They had food and could offer some sort of shelter and to me that was all that mattered. I wasn't pretty but I was a girl and the soldiers were all young men who had been away from their girlfriends in Russia for a long time and didn't know if they would ever get back. They talked it over and agreed that they could take me with them for a while.

I travelled with them to the next village but before we

212

went into the village they hid me in the back of one of the lorries. They loaded up what they had come to collect, boxes, ammunition I think, and then they pulled out. Once we were out of the village they stopped. The corporal climbed into the back and told me that now we would have sex. I was a virgin, completely without experience, but I knew it had to be done so I pulled down my underwear, lifted my skirt and lay down as the lorry started again and bumped along the road. When the corporal tried to push into me I cried out in pain and he stopped. The corporal banged on the back of the cab and the lorry stopped. The corporal got out and I heard the men talking, then the corporal came back. By this time I was crying. He told me to get out of the lorry. I thought they would leave me or kill me but when I got out they all looked at me kindly. The corporal asked my name and my age and asked me to tell them about myself. When I finished telling them they talked for a while and then told me that they would take me to the place they were going and hand me over to an officer. If I told the officer that I was eighteen and could drive a lorry then I might be allowed to join up. It was that or be left where I was on the road. It was all they could do for me, a chance. Did I want to take it?

What could I say? I said yes. We all got back into the lorries. I sat in the cab beside the corporal. He started the lorry and made me take the wheel. He sat close beside me so he could help me and straight away he began to teach me to drive. I knew I had to learn so I made myself do it and by the time we reached the place where we were going I could manage to give an imitation of someone who understood the rudiments of driving a lorry. There were many soldiers in the village where we stopped, and lorries and a few tanks. No one took any notice of me as the corporal took me to a building to see an officer. The officer I was taken to listened to the corporal who told him I was a farmer's daughter who could drive. He said my family were dead and I had asked

213

them to bring me with them so I could join up. The officer wasn't interested in me, he had a bandage round his head with a dark stain at the side and looked terrible, as if he hadn't slept for days. He asked me a few questions, name, age, where I had lived, nothing of any importance. Then told me I had joined the Red Army. He sent me with another soldier to get a uniform and that was that. I was a driver in the Red Army.

Those soldiers who had taken me in their lorries had saved my life and in return I served the Soviets with all my heart. For weeks it was a mess, full retreat and constant bombardment and air attacks. But I survived and got back to Russia where I fought on. Twice I was wounded and twice I recovered and returned to the fighting. After one year I was a corporal myself and by the time it was all coming to an end in 1945 I was a sergeant working with a specialist group.

Our job was taking art from occupied German museums and galleries and moving it back into Poland so it could be sent back to the Soviet Union. One day I was given orders to take two lorries and pick up some pictures from a chateau. It was a special job. The chateau had belonged to a top Nazi who had a big collection of stolen art. My orders were signed personally by a high Soviet functionary. They could not be questioned by anyone in the military. There were two lists of pictures. One list had thirty pictures that we were to crate up, put into one lorry and send on its way back to Poland. There were seventeen pictures on the second list. These had to be crated by me and my co-driver and loaded onto a lorry I would drive. Once these pictures were loaded and ready to go I had been told to open another envelope which contained a second set of orders.

We loaded the pictures as we were instructed, then I opened the envelope. It was an order signed by the same high functionary to take my load to Switzerland and see that

214

they were deposited in a bank in Zurich under the name of the functionary who had signed the orders. There would be no difficulties, they were expected by the bank, all arrangements had already been made. Also in the envelope was a diplomatic pass and some Swiss francs.

I set the other lorry off on its way back to Poland and me and my co-driver got going. The co-driver asked where we were headed and I told him. He didn't care, in fact he said that if we made it all the way and he liked Switzerland it might be worth thinking about taking up permanent residence and we both laughed. There were no problems on the journey, we stayed in the east of Germany and headed for Austria so we were in Soviet-controlled territory all along the route. All we had to do was show our orders and we were made welcome and then helped on our way. About ten kilometres from the Swiss border I told the co-driver who was at the wheel to stop. He stopped and I shot him through the head. I pushed his body out into the deserted road and drove on.

There was no trouble at the border, everything went well. Once in Switzerland I drove on to the first big place I came to. It was called St Gallen. There I used some of the money I'd been given to store the lorry in a secure garage then buy some civilian clothes. I looked around St Gallen until I found a place that sold paintings. It was a furniture shop, quite a big one and prosperous-looking. The sort of place where the well-off would buy things. I spoke to the man who owned the shop. I told him I was a Polish refugee. I said I came from a respectable family of modest wealth. I had got out of Poland but needed money. I had one small picture which my father had said was very valuable, a Corot. Would he look at it and perhaps buy it from me? He agreed to look at it. I went back to my garage, took one small picture from the lorry, un-crated it and wrapped it in some cloth and then in newspaper. It looked like an ordinary

215

parcel. I took it to the shop owner. He asked me questions about it, he was not a dishonest man. I told him my name was Sarah Perlmann, we had lived in Baranowicze and my father was a merchant who had collected art. He listened to me as I described Sarah's house and her father's collection. I told him about the picture I had brought him, a rural riverside scene painted around 1865 called Le Pont d'Avray. I said my father had bought it from a dealer while on a visit to Paris in 1928. I had no papers to support any of what I told him but he believed me, that the picture was truly mine, and agreed to buy it for what seemed to me a small fortune. I handed over the picture and he handed over the money. The reason he believed me was because I had seen that very painting hanging in the drawing room of Sarah's house many times, it was one of her favourites. Everything I had told the dealer, Sarah had told me. She loved it and the Nazis had stolen it from her father and from her and taken it back to Germany. I had recognised it as soon as I had seen it at the chateau. How funny that I should have been given the job of stealing it from the Germans for the Soviet State. And now a high Soviet functionary had arranged for me to steal it from the State so he could have it. So many thieves. And I had become like them. I had stolen it from them all.

After selling the painting I had plenty of money and bought a good forged passport. That was not so hard to do in those times. Many people needed passports and there were plenty of people who could supply them if you could pay. I had my paintings moved by rail to Genoa. In Genoa I arranged for me and my paintings to go to London. Everything was in chaos but if you had money and a good passport everything could be arranged. I went to London because I spoke English and I thought it would be safer than anywhere else in Europe. In London I told the same story and sold two more of Sarah's father's paintings. That was as many as I dared sell, any more and I would attract too much

216

attention. But there was more than enough money from the two paintings to plan carefully what I wanted to do. I wanted to get far away from the war and from Europe, but the paintings were a big problem. In Genoa no one had cared what was in my crates so long as I paid. London was not like that, questions would be asked, crates opened. The authorities were always on the lookout for contraband and for anything that might be stolen. I needed to be able to move them without any trouble from the authorities. I decided to have them disguised, painted over. But for that I knew I needed a real artist, someone who knew what they were doing, who would know how to cover them without destroying the original paintings. I also needed an artist who would do what I asked for payment and then keep his mouth shut. I went to several galleries but found nothing until I went into a gallery in Bond Street. Although it was in Bond Street it wasn't much of a place, small and up on the first floor. There I saw three paintings which were truly hideous, how anyone could paint such things was beyond me and I was sure that no one in their right mind would give money for them. But the artist might be the man I was looking for. If this was what he was trying to sell then he must need money. The three pictures were very big and were described as studies for figures at the base of a crucifixion. They were like nothing I had seen before, meaningless, awful things, but they gave me an idea, the perfect way to hide my paintings and be sure that no one would take any interest in the pictures that covered them. The painter was a man called Francis Bacon. I told the gallery I wanted to meet him to discuss a commission and they arranged it.

He was a strange man, driven in some way and at once passionate but detached. He listened to what I wanted and to my surprise he agreed. I think he had his own reasons for wanting to paint what I asked of him. I handed over the remaining fourteen pictures. Bacon said he wouldn't paint over my pictures, that would destroy them. He would re-canvas over the original paintings and do his work on that. His work on the paintings took just over a year, I kept in touch but never saw the work until it was finished. It was exactly what I wanted. They were truly awful, hideous, revolting. No one would want such things, yet he seemed pleased with them, proud. He said that they would be his secret masterpiece, perhaps the greatest works he would ever do. And he laughed, he said it was wonderful. A great, wonderful, secret joke. I didn't understand him, but I didn't care. As I said, he was a strange man. I paid him what we had agreed. He didn't sign any of the pictures but he gave me a signed letter of authenticity naming and dating the pictures. I had them crated and booked a passage to Canada. The authorities were on the look-out for anything that might be war loot being moved through British ports and the crates were all opened and the paintings checked before loading. But it was as I had arranged and once they saw that they were Catholic Stations of the Cross, recently painted religious works, and I had a letter showing my ownership there was no problem.

I moved to Canada, to a small town in Alberta. I still had enough money but it wouldn't last forever so I bought a house, put my pictures into one of the bedrooms and set about starting a business. All I knew was transport, lorries and driving, so I bought a good second-hand lorry and began a transport business. I found I was good at it, my Red Army training had made me perfect for the job. After six years I had four lorries and after ten years a fleet of twelve but I never forgot my pictures. I knew almost nothing about art but I was learning a lot about storage and it didn't take long for me to decide that if the pictures stayed too long in a bedroom in crates they might become irreparably damaged. I needed them to be where they could be looked after. They were devotional works so the obvious choice was a Catholic

Church. To keep my pictures safe I loaned them to the local parish church. The priest didn't want them. I didn't blame him, they were shocking things. But I told him that I had saved them from the Nazis, that they were commissioned by my father for the local church where we lived in the Sudetenland but the Nazis in the congregation had objected saying they were decadent filth. How can the depiction of the sufferings of Jesus be filth, I asked him? I told him that the rejection suffered by my father at the hands of his parish church made me give up the practice of my faith. But if he took the pictures I would feel able to come to church again. After that he couldn't refuse, to reject them would make him no better than the Nazis, and as I was prepared to make a fat donation if he let them hang in his church, he took them. The parishioners were shocked, but when it was explained they accepted them. Once they were up I started to go to church on Sundays and, as far as the world was concerned, I was a Catholic returned to the fold. It wasn't hard. I went and did what everyone else did, no one bothered me and I bothered no one. My pictures were safe so I got on with my life.

The business kept on growing, more lorries, longer runs, bigger contracts. After twenty years I had one of the biggest haulage and storage firms in central Canada and I decided that now I was wealthy enough it was time to go back to my pictures. I took them from the church saying that I wanted them cleaned. I found a man who could take the Stations off the works under them without harming either picture. I photographed the stolen pieces and then had the Stations put back over them and returned to the church. I paid the man well, very well, but he was greedy and tried to blackmail me. He had seen the pictures and guessed they were stolen and probably war loot. He threatened to go to the authorities. What could I do? I met him, gave him some money, and while he was checking it I shot him through the head. I took *back the money and left him to be found. It was a lonely stretch of road and we'd met by night. No one saw anything and there was nothing anyone knew to connect me to the man. I waited. If he had written anything down and the police found it they would come and I would tell them what had happened. But no one came. After six weeks I set off for London. I told everyone that I was taking an extended holiday in England. I deserved a break after so many years' hard work.*

I wanted to go to London to find out about my stolen pictures, how valuable they were, what their history was. Where had they come from before the Nazis took them? But when I got to London I found that Francis Bacon was becoming famous as an artist, very famous. The middle of the Canadian prairie is a long way from the art world and no one in the church took any notice any more of my Stations. But to leave them out in the open was too much of a risk. One day they would be noticed and questions asked. I returned to Canada immediately and said I had decided that I didn't want a vacation, I wanted to retire. I was going to sell the business, sell up altogether and move away. I would, of course, be taking my father's Stations with me. The priest wasn't sad to see them go.

I decided I would go as far west as I could and chose Vancouver. Selling the business made me a wealthy woman and I was able to settle comfortably in a new home in a new city. But I had to find a new place for my pictures, somewhere Catholic but where no-one would see them who might realise what they were. I found the convent and offered them the pictures with the same story and again with the offer of a fat donation and again they were accepted.

And there they stayed and I began the project I had worked all those years for. I took up oil painting, I paid well for lessons and was not only taught how to paint, at which I was very bad, but also how to mount and frame a canvas and how to do some basic restoration. While I was learning my new trade I quietly researched where the pictures had come from before they were looted. It wasn't easy, it was before the internet made such research fast and simple. I had made friends in the art world of Vancouver, friends who had reference books and weren't surprised if I asked about certain pictures. I was a wealthy, retired middle-aged woman who had taken up a hobby and let it become a passion. I managed to find out a great deal over the years, why not? I gave my whole time to it. Three of the paintings were from art galleries in European cities. I took the Stations over those three from the convent saying I wanted them checked for cleaning. I removed the originals, re-framed the Stations and returned them to the convent. The original paintings I sent back to the galleries anonymously. I tried to trace more owners, but in ten years I found only one more. The nephew of a man who had died in the camps. He lived with his family in Nebraska. I sent him his picture with a brief note. The rest stayed in the convent. It became clear to me that the work of restoration of the paintings to their rightful owners could and probably would take many years and I was not getting any younger. Although I was well over sixty years old I applied to adopt a child. Adoption it seemed was no different from anything else. In Genoa, in London, in Alberta, all it took to get round any problems was enough money and I had plenty. I adopted a boy. I saw to it that he had everything, a good home, a good education, all a child needed. When he was twenty-one I told him about the pictures and that it would be his job to find the owners I had been unable to trace. He was wonderful. In five years he had returned three more pictures. When I die, I promised myself, the work I did would go on through my son. The last right of victims is restitution and it will be made, for Sarah's sake.

There was one more page. On it was hand-written:

221

The Last Will and Testament of Anna Sikora, born Miriam Feldstein. I leave the Francis Bacon pictures of the Stations of the Cross to the convent of the Sisters of Perpetual Prayer, Vancouver. Under ten of these paintings are some stolen works which I now turn over to the Canadian authorities with the wish that, if possible, their rightful owners be found and their property returned. If that proves impossible then that they be dealt with in whichever way the authorities think fit.

Everything else I own, the whole balance of my estate, I leave to Mary Jackson who has been my friend and companion for the last ten years.

Under the writing there was the printed name of Anna Sikora followed by her signature, then the printed name of Miriam Feldstein followed by the signature. It was dated yesterday. Below the signatures and the date was written, *witnessed by*, followed by a blank space. Jimmy put the sheet of paper on the table and put the other pages back in the envelope. He went and got a pen, came back and signed the will in the space for the witness's signature, then he put the final page back with the others and took the envelope into the bedroom and put it in his holdall. He went back into the living room and sat down beside his cold tea.

She must have written the will after he had left her yesterday and she'd realised her son had sold the three paintings he'd said he'd returned and pocketed the money. She knew what her son would do, that she was next on his list. It isn't too hard to kill a ninety-year-old and make it look natural. A pillow over the face and it looks like a peaceful death. And who would look into it? She was a determined woman though, she'd made sure that her will was in the hands of someone who would see that it got where it needed to go. The son, even if he got away with her murder, would get nothing from the estate. The phone rang. Jimmy looked at his watch, half-past five.

'Yes?'

'It's Reception, Mr Costello, there's someone to see you. I thought I'd phone and ask before I said you were in.'

'I'm in.'

'Thank you.'

Jimmy went back to his chair and waited. A few minutes later there was a knock at his door.

'Who is it?'

'It's Laura Lawrence, Mr Costello. I think you wanted to see me.'

So this was it. Jimmy got up, crossed the room and opened the door.

Laura Lawrence was standing there looking just the same, except Jimmy knew the truth now. Dark hair and glasses, holding a handbag. Jimmy guessed it held a knife, a gun would be too noisy and silencers weren't easy to come by, and he didn't think Lawrence would try to do it by strangling him. It would be a knife alright.

'Come in, Mr Sikora, I've been waiting for you.'

Jimmy turned and took a couple of steps. He heard the door close and then felt the knife go into his back about halfway down his ribs. He jerked forward and the knife came out. He turned, he was hurt but he was upright. He made a fist and lifted his hand. Lawrence Sikora stepped forward and Jimmy hit him hard, but on the nose, it would slow him down but it wouldn't stop him. Lawrence stepped forward and the knife went in again, just under the heart, and Jimmy fell to the floor. He was probably dead before he hit it.

Sikora threw the knife into the open handbag and put his hand to his bleeding nose. The bridge of his glasses had broken and the pieces lay at his feet. He stooped down and put the handbag on the floor and pulled out a tissue which he held to his nose. He checked the body. The wounds had started bleeding heavily, there was blood on the carpet but none of it was his. He had got the hand to his nose in time. He put the pieces of his glasses into the handbag, closed it and stood up. He looked around. He had touched nothing and left no traces. If anyone asked, he had a nose-bleed. He gave the body one last look then went to the door. When he opened it Inspector Brownlow and Constable Liu were facing him. He stood looking at them. Liu looked past him into the room then pushed past and went to the body, stooped down, examined it then stood up.

'He's dead.'

Inspector Brownlow reached under his jacket and pulled out a pair of handcuffs, as he did so, Lawrence saw the gun on his belt.

'Lawrence Sikora, I arrest you for the murder of James Costello. You are not obliged to say anything...'

Sikora was handcuffed as his rights were read and the blood from his nose ran down to his chin and dripped onto the carpet. He said nothing and was led away. Liu made a phone call. He would wait with the body until the crime scene unit arrived. There was nothing else to do. Jimmy had made sure everything was ready. The right blood was on the carpet now and Sikora would stand trial for at least one murder. It wasn't what Liu had wanted but it had been what Jimmy wanted, Sikora facing a murder charge that he couldn't beat. That was what counted.

Chapter Thirty-Seven

Professor McBride had taken a suite at the Rosedale on Robson when she'd arrived from Rome the previous day and immediately asked for a meeting with either of the officers who had made the arrest. She'd made the right calls before she'd left Rome and Liu had been the one who turned up. They sat in the bar of the hotel, Liu had a beer and she had a glass of red wine. It was mid-afternoon and the place wasn't very busy. Liu had obviously been told to co-operate, that she was someone with the right kind of friends. The sort the police are more than happy to co-operate with.

'He phoned Brownlow, told him that he had located Laura Lawrence and had arranged to meet her. He said we should wait in the lobby of the hotel from five onwards. When she arrived we were to follow her to his room and wait outside the door until he called us in and we'd get all the evidence we needed to nail Lawrence for murder. Brownlow didn't like it but Jimmy told him that it had to be his way or not at all. If Brownlow didn't agree he'd scrub the meeting and make it another time and another place and if Brownlow tried to pick her up in the lobby Jimmy would make sure any evidence he gave would become confused, so confused it might be useless. Brownlow wasn't happy but what could he do? Jimmy had all the cards, he'd found this Lawrence woman and he'd set up the meeting. We desperately needed to talk to her, our investigation into Sr Lucy Gray's killing was going nowhere, so Brownlow agreed. We were in the bar by five, sitting where we had a good view of the lobby and reception. At half past a woman matching Laura Lawrence's description came in and went to the desk. Of course, as it turns out, she was actually Lawrence Sikora in disguise. The desk clerk made a call and she went to the elevators. We went to the desk and the clerk said she'd asked for Mr Costello so we went up, went to his room and waited for Jimmy to call us in. He didn't call us in but he kept his side of the deal. We got the evidence he wanted us to have.'

'Was there much evidence of a struggle?'

'No, not much. Jimmy took a stab wound to the back which wouldn't have been immediately fatal, got in at least one punch, then took the blade to his heart and that was that.'

'What will happen to Lawrence Sikora?'

'I'm not sure.'

'Not sure? You both walked into the room where he had just murdered someone. How can you not be sure?'

'Because he's very clever. He admits killing Costello but claims that he did it because Costello was blackmailing his mother and he believed that the stress caused by the blackmail brought on her death. His solicitor claims the state of his mind was disturbed by her death and by the cause of her death.'

'Would it be a defence?'

'No, probably not, but it might get the charge reduced. It's hard to tell, it all depends on what evidence he can bring forward and what evidence we can put against it.'

'Does he have any evidence?'

'A note in Jimmy's handwriting to his mother. The evidence of Mary the housekeeper that Mrs Sikora met with Jimmy and after he left she seemed agitated. That Mrs Sikora and her son spoke later that day and there was some sort of argument, and that when the son left Mrs Sikora was very distressed. The next morning Jimmy came back and when he found Mrs Sikora was dead told Mary that he'd now have to deal with the son and she should give him the note. That's all we've been given so far.'

'All circumstantial but, put together like that, it's quite a lot.'

'Like I say, unless we can put something up against it, he might have enough to get the charge changed to manslaughter and maybe plead guilty but with diminished responsibility. With a good lawyer he might not serve much time at all. We're working on it.'

'I see. What does Mr Sikora say about the pictures?'

'Claims he never knew anything about them until she told him about the blackmail.'

'And about going to the hotel?'

'He says that after he'd accompanied his mother's body to the funeral parlour and arranged for his mother's funeral he decided to go and confront Costello. He admits to putting a knife in the handbag but says he had no intention of using it. It was for self-protection. If Costello was confronted he thought he might turn violent. He said he told Costello he knew about the blackmail and that he blamed him for his mother's death and that he was going to go to the police. Costello hit him and he defended himself. They struggled and Costello got stabbed.'

'But the disguise? The business of dressing up like a woman? If he was disguised that means premeditation surely?'

'He says it wasn't a disguise. He says he often dresses as a woman, that anyone at the gay Outreach Programme will confirm that. He says he does it in times of stress or confusion, it's a method of release.'

'And the lies about being a postgraduate student?'

'He didn't want anyone at the chaplaincy to know who he really was. His mother knew nothing about his cross-dressing, she wouldn't have understood, and he couldn't explain so he made up the postgraduate story to make sure

227

that she would never know.'

'A bit elaborate, surely?'

'He says he was afraid that if anyone found out she was wealthy they might try to blackmail him.'

'Blackmail again?'

'Oh, yes. The way he tells it he's an inadequate mummy's boy who is ashamed of his dressing-up and always afraid of being found out. He wants to come across as a sad, confused man who has no employment and lives at home with his mother, not the dangerous, multiple killer type. We talked to a couple of people from the Outreach Programme and as far as I can see his story will hold up. Like I say, he's clever, he's built himself a story that may work and he's going to stick to it. He may still be tried for murder but it's not certain. The charge may have to be reduced to be sure of getting a conviction and even if he's found guilty I don't know how long he'll get. If he gets a good lawyer who can make a good case for diminished responsibility he may only get a few years.'

'What about the mother? What was the cause of death?'

'Her heart gave out. It could have been brought on by suffocation but it could have been natural causes.'

They sat for a moment, neither seemed to want the drinks on the table in front of them.

'What will happen to the pictures?'

'The old ones or the new ones?'

'Both.'

'I don't know. No one seems to know. The new ones will go to Sikora unless she left them to someone else, which I doubt. The old ones, the valuable ones, well, who do they really belong to? No one knows how she came to have them or why she hid them under the new stuff. We'll trace them as best we can but how do you find the rightful owners after all this time? It's possible he may get those as well. From a straightforward killing it's turning into a mess.'

'What about the other killings?'

'What about them? Costello was the only one who said they were linked. Brinkmeyer committed suicide. That hasn't changed. The art dealer is missing, we have no body. A nun in London got hit by a car. Mrs Sikora died of old age. Only the nun who ran the outreach was actually murdered and we have no evidence of who was responsible. Costello knew we couldn't make a case even for an arrest never mind get a conviction.'

'So he set himself up in a way that Sikora couldn't get out of?'

'Yes, except Sikora is cleverer than Costello thought and he might very well not go down for murder. Hell, with a really good lawyer he might even get off.'

'What about Mr Costello's effects?'

'What about them?'

'When can you release them?'

'They're not evidence and the suite's been cleared as a crime scene. We've no interest in it any more. I suppose whatever happens to his things would be between you and the hotel once we get a signature to say who got them.'

'When can the body be released?'

'In a couple of days. Does he have any relatives?'

'He may have, somewhere.' It wasn't a lie exactly, it was a manipulation of the truth. He had a daughter and grandchildren in Australia, but next of kin at this point would be an unnecessary complication and she wanted to get back to Rome 'Will his belongings be released with the body?'

'They're not needed, you can have them whenever you want unless the hotel wants to hold them against the unpaid bill. A signature is all we'll want to say it's no longer anything to do with us.'

'Yes, there's always paperwork. No, I don't think I want his belongings. You can dispose of them.'

229

'It would be easier if we could release them to someone. That way we get a signature.'

'Very well, I'll come and sign for them tomorrow morning.

Professor McBride stood up. So did Liu.

'Thank you, Detective.'

She held out her one arm and they shook hands. 'You've been very helpful.'

Liu nodded an acknowledgement and McBride walked out of the bar into the lobby and headed for the elevators.

Chapter Thirty-Eight

Once back in her suite McBride put her handbag on the table, opened it and pulled out an envelope. It was addressed to her at the Collegio. She took out the pages, sat down and re-read them.

Professor McBride,

By the time you get this I will be dead. I will have been murdered by the man who killed Sr Philomena. He will be in custody and will stand trial for my murder. If I'm lucky he'll get life. He was clever and ruthless. Leaving me out of it, he killed five people including his adoptive mother and there was no way anyone could have arrested him for any of the killings with any hope of getting a conviction. There was only one way to get him so I took it. Sikora is clever, he'll try to worm his way out of my death, I don't know how, but he will. Whatever story he tells, let him tell it. Let him bury himself with it. When the case goes to court I want you to give something to the police. It's a brown envelope with some hand-written pages in it. I don't want anyone to know about it until just before the trial when Sikora can't change his story. It's in my holdall. It's nothing to do with my killing so it should still be there. One way or another make sure that it stays safe until it's needed. I was given it by Mrs Sikora the day before she died. I read it for the first time the next day as soon as I got back from her house where I saw the son, spoke to the housekeeper and realised what was going on. I knew he'd have to come after me as soon as he saw the note I'd given to his mother. Once I'd read Mrs.

231

Sikora's story I knew that, whatever he came up with, the contents of the envelope would finish him. It proves he knew about the pictures and the police may even be able to prove he sold three of them. And there's a bonus, a will. I doubt it will stand up in any court but it will blow any loving son act he puts on out of the water.

Now to other things.

Get in touch with a man called Ian Cross in London, maybe he's retired but you should still be able to reach him through Barnaby, Cresswell and Partners. They're accountants in the City. Tell him to liquidate everything and put it in the Swiss account. Can you arrange to sell up everything in Rome and put the money in my Rome account? The pass book's in my apartment. Also in my apartment is a will in which I have made you my executor. I had it drawn up after I got back from Santander. I knew then I was finished, I just didn't know how or when I would go so I wanted to be ready. When it's all done, send all the money to my daughter in Australia. Tell her it's for her and the kids, that Bernie would have wanted them to have it.

As for me, have a Mass said, light a few candles and get me into the ground somewhere.

James Cornelius Costello.

She put the letter on her lap. So that was the end of Jimmy Costello.

She looked at the letter again. It was clever, keep the killer punch until it couldn't be avoided or deflected. Hide it from the police and you could hide it from the defence until it was too late. It would be admitted as evidence only when, as Jimmy put it, Sikora had buried himself with his own story. Damn, he was going to be hard to replace. The world didn't stop just because one man decided it was time for him to get off.

She phoned reception and asked to speak to the manager.

'I will settle Mr Costello's bill and I will sign the police release and take charge and remove all of his belongings. If you would have them packed up and store them here at the hotel until I can arrange what is to be done with them?' The manager was happy to do anything she asked. It was bad enough having someone murdered in your hotel, but it was worse if they were murdered with their bill unpaid and the room stayed out of action. If Professor McBride was going to settle up he was going to agree to anything she asked. 'I'd like to look at Mr Costello's suite, please, and I would like you to accompany me.'

The manager said he'd be right up.

The manager looked out of the window. He didn't want to see what she was doing, he didn't want to know. He wanted it finished. Professor McBride looked at the bloodstains on the carpet. The manager watched her in the reflection of the glass but said nothing. She went into the bedroom and checked the wardrobes. There wasn't much in the way of clothes to pack, enough for one suitcase probably. The black holdall was in the bottom of the wardrobe. She nudged it open with her foot. It was empty except for the envelope. She went back into the living room.

'Clear it out, pack it up and give it all to any charity that will take it. Get someone to check if there are any more papers. There should be a report somewhere. If there are any papers at all, put them with his passport and wallet and keep them in the hotel safe until I can get round to picking them up.'

'It would be better if you took charge of all the...'

'Do you want his bill settled and the room vacated? I should think you'd be quite keen to have it empty so you could at least change the carpet.'

The manager capitulated. He was indeed desperate to change the carpet.

'I'll arrange it.'

'Good, that's all then.'

They left the suite. In the lift going down, Professor McBride ordered one more favour from him.

'I need an undertaker. Get one to call me tomorrow morning before ten and tell him I'll need a Catholic priest for a funeral at some point. I'll probably be leaving the day after tomorrow and I have a busy schedule so please make sure it's all done as I ask.'

The manager agreed. He didn't like her. Maybe it was the fact that she was black or maybe it was because she only had one arm, but whatever it was he felt a little frightened of her. He wanted her gone and out of his hotel as much as he wanted the blood-stained carpet gone, so things could get back to normal.

The next morning the phone rang in her suite at ten past nine.

'Yes, that's right. The police are holding a body, that of James Cornelius Costello. When it is ready to be released I want you to collect it and arrange for its burial. Did you contact a Catholic priest? Good. When you have the body, arrange for a Catholic burial, a Mass and light three candles. It doesn't matter what religion you are, put a few coins in the box and light three candles. Add it to the bill. There will be no-one at the funeral so it can take place at any time the priest wishes. I am leaving for Rome tomorrow morning so by four this afternoon have the bill ready and I will pay it in advance. Thank you.'

She then phoned the police station and asked for Detective Liu.

'I am coming to the police station to sign the necessary papers. Have them ready for me in half an hour.'

She put the phone down, left her suite and headed for the police station.

When she got there Liu came out to her. She signed the papers and told him the name of the undertaker who would come for the body when it was released.

'Tell me, Detective, has Mr Sikora made a full statement?'

'Yes.'

'And his lawyer will proceed with the defence along the lines you told me about yesterday, grief and stress caused by his mother's death?'

'Yes, it looks that way.'

'And no knowledge whatsoever of any stolen art works?'

'No, he still denies any knowledge.'

'Could he change his story now if new evidence came to light?'

'It would depend on the evidence but he's got his story pretty well fixed.'

'There were some papers in Mr Costello's suite. I asked the manager to put them in the hotel safe. I don't know what they are but you should read them just in case they have any bearing on the case.'

'What sort of papers?'

'You're the detective, not me. You work out what they are and then do with them what you wish.'

And she left.

In the taxi back to the hotel she went over things.

The Diocese of Vancouver did not own nor had it ever owned any war-time loot. The last person to have had possession of the pictures was dead, murdered by her adopted son. The paintings, what was left of them, were totally unconnected with the Church and were someone else's problem. Her problem was how to replace Costello. He was a difficult man alive and it seemed he was almost as difficult dead. Still, it shouldn't be any more of a problem to clean up the Rome end than it had been here. Once she had settled with the hotel and the undertaker, she was finished, she could go back to Rome. The only question was, did she get a good night's sleep and fly out tomorrow morning or go this evening and try to sleep on the plane.

The question wasn't an easy one, it lasted all the way to her hotel.

Postscript

'Mr. Cross, Mr Ian Cross?'

'Yes?'

'Mr James Costello asked me to contact you.'

There was a silence for a moment.

'I don't know any James Costello.'

'I see. But I'll pass on the message anyway.'

McBride waited but the phone at the other end didn't go dead.

'If you want to, but I still don't know any James Costello.'

'You are to liquidate everything and put the money into the Swiss account.'

'That means nothing to me.'

'Of course it doesn't, and you don't know Mr Costello. I must have the wrong man. However, just as an academic point, I'm afraid I know nothing about Swiss banks, nor how long it would take to liquidate assets, get them into a Swiss bank and available as cleared funds. Think of it as an academic enquiry.'

'Two to three weeks to make cleared funds available if they are held in a form that is easily liquidated, bonds, shares, things like that. If it's something else you're thinking of doing I can't help, I'm semi-retired and won't be taking on any new clients.'

'No, I don't need financial help or advice and I'm sure all your present clients value your work for them. I'm sure if Mr Costello had been your client he would have been totally confident you would handle his affairs exactly as he would have wished. Well, thank you for your time and the information you have given me. I suppose the Swiss account will be checked in three weeks by whoever does look after Mr Costello's financial affairs to see that what he wants has been done. If no money has been deposited I dare say the matter will be followed up in some way. But that, of course, would be nothing to do with you. Goodbye.'

In the City of London a senior semi-retired partner at a well-respected and old-established firm of accountants surprised his long-serving secretary by declaring, at ten thirty in the morning, that some urgent business had come up and he had to go out and attend to it at once. He said he would not be returning to the office as he felt a little unwell and once his business was finished he would go home. He wanted no calls or messages at all during the day, no matter what happened. She would have to deal with appointments as best she could. He then left the building. His secretary, after his sudden departure, was a little worried, he certainly didn't look well. She wondered for a moment whether he might not have had some bad news, but then returned to her work and began to make a series of phone calls cancelling appointments and explaining that Mr Cross was, unfortunately, indisposed today and would not be in his office.

In Rome Professor McBride thought about her phone conversation. Mr Cross had been properly careful and cautious but not able to keep out of his voice the fact that he was frightened. She suspected that if he had been told Jimmy was dead he would still have been careful and cautious and when she checked the Swiss account might very well discover that Mr Cross had suddenly become richer by however much he handled for Jimmy. Not that she cared one way or another. Jimmy had come by his wealth from a life of violence and corruption, if it was taken by someone else who could do it without violence or

238

corruption, why not? Still, she had done what Jimmy wanted and would see to it that his money reached his daughter and her family. She owed him that much, to get his money to his grandchildren. He had worked very well for her. She looked at the papers on her desk. A will naming her executor, a passport which lay open with Jimmy staring blankly out at her and a pass-book for a bank account which held thirty-eight thousand Euros. His apartment was empty and up for sale and the contents had been removed, sorted and either sold off or given to charity. What lay on her desk and in a grave in some Vancouver cemetery was all that was left of James Cornelius Costello.

She opened a drawer, swept the papers in, closed it and turned to look out of the window towards the distant hills of Frascati. They were invisible, hidden by clouds from which heavy rain had been falling all morning. She spoke to the invisible hills.

'Well, Jimmy, you chose a bad time to get off the whirligig. Things don't stop just because you decide that it's time to find out what, if anything, comes next. Goodbye, Jimmy.'

And she mouthed in silence the ancient Catholic formula they had both known all their lives.

'May the souls of the faithful departed, through the mercy of God, rest in peace. Amen.'

The Road to Redemption Series

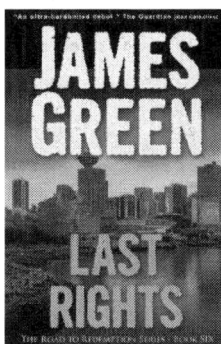

Meet Jimmy Costello.

Quiet, respectable, God-fearing family man? Or thuggish
street-fighter with a past full of dark secrets? Perhaps the
answer is somewhere in between…

Á

Proudly published by Accent Press

www.accentpress.co.uk

28357021R00149

Printed in Great Britain
by Amazon